Praise for L ... Dane's
Once and Again

"Readers will be smitten by the Southern charm of this sexy starter to the Petal, GA, series. The sensual romance between these likable protagonists, the focus on family, and ample rolls in the hay make for an entertaining read for your contemporary set."

> ~ *Library Journal*

"Lauren Dane is so talented and creative when it comes to character development. She brings to the forefront the perfections and the flaws of each of her engaging characters... This short story is so full of emotion that you can't help but deeply feel every little twist and turn."

> ~ *Long and Short Reviews*

"The strength of character and love between them had me turning the pages, not wanting to put their story down. *Once and Again* is a love story totally in keeping with today's lives – hot and passionate with the reality of pain and chaos."

> ~ *Joyfully Reviewed*

"This was a great story and I can't wait for more of Lauren Dane's talented work."

> ~ *Fallen Angel Reviews*

Look for these titles by
Lauren Dane

Now Available:

Once and Again

Lauren Dane

SAMHAIN
PUBLISHING

Samhain Publishing, Ltd.
11821 Mason Montgomery Road, 4B
Cincinnati, OH 45249
www.samhainpublishing.com

Once and Again
Copyright © 2012 by Lauren Dane
Print ISBN: 978-1-60928-822-8
Digital ISBN: 978-1-60928-520-3

Editing by Anne Scott
Cover by Kendra Egert

First Samhain Publishing, Ltd. electronic publication: August 2011
First Samhain Publishing, Ltd. print publication: September 2012

Dedication

This one is for all the fans of my Chase Brothers who've encouraged me to make a return visit for one of Tate's siblings.

And for Eileen, who was the inspiration for Polly Chase. I miss you every day.

Chapter One

Lily wandered through her new home—the apartment above the garage. Hard to fully think of it as home when just two weeks ago it'd been a collection place for unwanted crap her mother refused to get rid of.

She looked at herself in the mirror one last time before heading to the house to grab her brother. She didn't have a suit or anything, but she used what she had. She'd come to realize appearances were indeed important when it came to dealing with authority figures. These were Chris's teachers and his principal, their support would go a long way in helping him get where he needed to be.

Competent. Yes, that was it. She wasn't Chris's mom and she was still relatively young, so she wanted to appear competent. Solid. A together, trustworthy adult sibling pitching in to get Chris back on track at school. Lily thought she might have nailed it. Enough to do the job anyway.

And, she thought as she took another look, perhaps it was petty, but she thought she also looked good enough that when she had to deal with Nathan, he'd see what he'd been missing.

Not that she'd put any thought into how he might react when she saw him again after so many years. Or what he felt in general. Much.

Of course the snort of amusement might have ruined that statement.

Taking a deep breath she went down and saw the box she'd told Chris to carry up to her place still sitting next to the car.

"Chris! Get over here and take this box."

"I don't see why you didn't just hire someone to do this," he muttered. But he did it, carrying the box upstairs with care to keep those grumbles under his breath.

He came back out quickly and she sent a smirk his way. "Why would I pay someone when I've got a perfectly good fifteen-year-old who can pick things up and move them?"

"For free!"

"Free? Ha! You cost a lot more than free, kid. In any case, you've got to step up your game. Helping out around the house is part of that."

Inside, their mother wandered around watering plants. It was as if there was no problem at all. Or hell, that they were even there really. Lily turned to her brother, stepping between him and their mother to interrupt his attention.

"Get your stuff, I'm taking you to school in fifteen minutes. You can look like a hobo, or you can clean yourself up. Either way you're in my car and we're leaving in *fifteen minutes.*"

"I heard you the first time. I get it. Fifteen minutes." His defiance didn't last long and he broke eye contact, dipping his chin. But he wasn't quite done. "Still don't see why you have to go with me."

"Let's establish up front just how not okay it is to talk to me with an attitude other than *yes ma'am.* As for your statement that you don't know why I have to go with you. Seems to me, Christopher, that's your problem in a nutshell. Wake your ass up and get yourself together before you end up pulling slurpees for people for the rest of your life." She looked at her watch. "I'm leaving this driveway in *fifteen minutes* and you will be in the car. Tick tock." She gently prodded him out of the room and finished the last bit of her own preparation as she gulped down her coffee.

Her mother came into the kitchen and began to clean up the nonexistent mess.

"I'm going to take him and then meet with his principal and as many teachers as I can. I should be back by noon or so, but you have my cell number if you need me." Lily checked her bag to be sure she had the folder of information she'd need.

"Oh is that today? All right then." Pamela Travis looked troubled for a moment and then smiled.

"Yes. And we can talk about it when I get back, all right?" Lily had actually hoped her mother would come with her to these meetings, but the strong woman Pamela might have been when her children were young had slowly fizzled out until she disappeared completely when Rodger had walked out.

Six months ago, right before the start of the school year, Lily's father up and announced he'd filed for divorce and was in the process of moving in with his new girlfriend. Emphasis on the girl. A twenty-year-old who'd babysat for Chris many times. Chris had called Lily right away, and she'd come to Petal to find her mother a wreck and her brother at loose ends.

Her father was just fine. As if there'd be any doubt he wouldn't be sure of that. The one person in Rodger Travis's life who got his consideration and time was Rodger Travis. This dumb hooker he'd shacked up with hadn't been the first, though she was probably the youngest. He'd left town and had been back exactly once to see his son.

Wasn't like Atlanta was the other side of the earth. No, it was an easy enough commute for him to make at least once a week. Too bad he was so wrapped up in banging a girl barely old enough to have graduated high school.

It wasn't really a surprise then, that in the wake of all this upset, her sweet little brother had started messing up big time. Things quickly got out of control. Cutting school. Bad grades and even, two weeks before, a trip to jail when he'd been busted drinking in the abandoned barn out on Summit Farm. Stupid.

Over drinks, at two in the morning, her mother had finally confessed the depth of the problem and her inability to handle Chris.

Lily had found out a number of things that night. First that her mother had turned increasingly to the numb reality of an entire bottle of wine with her anti-anxiety medication. Second, that her father wasn't interested in the mess he'd turned his wife into or the devastation his abandonment had brought to his son's life. When Lily had spoken to him, he'd helpfully suggested Lily take out a loan to send Chris to military school. Their older sister, Nancy, was an opportunistic, lazy bitch and would prove no help either. Which, to be fair, Lily had known since childhood.

Getting Chris back on track had fallen to Lily, even though she'd escaped Petal years ago and hoped not to look back.

She had to look back now.

Speaking of Chris... She looked at her watch. "Let's go!" She headed down the hall where she found him on his bed with a handheld video game system and his headphones on.

"You're not my mother," he said sullenly.

"No, I'm not. I'm your sister and I'm here because of the wreck you're making of your life. I love you and I'm here to put a stop to it. So. You can get up on your own and walk out, or I swear to you, Chris, I will show up in every single one of your classes and sit next to you to be sure you're there. Moreover, I will drag you by the back of the neck from one place to the next. I am not having it. Your little vacation from reality is over. Get. Your. Butt. In. The. Car. Now."

Grumbling, he still got a move on at last and headed toward the door. She took his book bag and gave it a look.

"Take this with you. I want you to know I will be checking your work so don't forget to bring it home each night. We'll be sure you have all the supplies you need and all that jazz."

"Great."

She laughed, pushing him with a guiding hand on his shoulder through the house and toward the driveway.

He raised a hand at their mother. "Bye, Mom!"

Her mother came into the room and kissed Chris's cheek. He blushed and hugged her back. He was a good kid; she knew that. He'd lost his way and now she'd help him find it again.

"Love you both," their mother called out.

She parked in the lot, noting that it looked pretty much the same as it had a decade before when she'd attended Petal High. The same mix of cars from shiny new to beater in the parking lot. The same kids hanging out and laughing before school started.

"Chris, I'm meeting with your principal right now, and she and I are going to talk about how we can work with you to get you passing this year, all right?"

He tried to look away, but she wouldn't let him. She took his shoulder and turned him to face her. "You can't do this anymore. Playtime is over. You're going to fail if you don't take care of your business. And that's not acceptable. If it was all you were capable of that would be one thing, but you're a smart kid. Don't blow it."

"If I have to hear all these lectures, I'd rather go to class."

She laughed and whacked him upside the head. "Whatever it takes, monkey-boy, whatever it takes. I'll see you after school. Right out here." She pointed to the parent pick-up lane.

"Until my car gets back from the shop, Mom's letting me

use hers. No need to pick me up."

This one she and her mother had only reached agreement on the day before when they'd gotten word Chris had cut fourth period again. One of the many reasons her mother had agreed to let Lily be in charge was her own seeming inability to give Chris hard consequences. Though Lily was beginning to think a big part of that had to do with the pills, but she hoped that would end soon too. In either case, there was a new sheriff in town and this was going to end one way or another. Starting with the removal of privileges like a car—a car Lily didn't think he'd done anything to earn to start with.

"Boy, did you hit your head? Who drove you in? I did. How is it you'll get Mom's car? Pay attention. Anyway, only boys who go to school and pass get cars their mothers pay for. Until you get your grades back above failing, you're not driving anything."

His eyes widened and his mouth hardened. He looked an awful lot like his oldest sister right about then, and that scared her enough to stay hard and on task with him.

"That's my car. You can't do that."

"Chris, you're missing the point. I can. I will. You've pushed Mom around long enough. Go to class or I'll escort you there myself." She kept it quiet, but made sure to keep eye contact with him.

"Fine."

She shrugged and stepped back. "See you at two fifty." Before he said another word, she moved past him and toward the administration offices.

"Lily Travis for Principal Bunton, please." She held on to her folder with all the letters, notifications, emails and other things the school had sent over the last semester.

Living with her mother and raising a nearly sixteen-year-old boy with a ferocious sense of entitlement. Just what she thought her life would be like at twenty-eight.

Nathan Murphy had been grading a test when the knock on his door startled him. A warning that he wasn't seeing any students just then died on his lips when he looked up and saw...*her* standing there.

Long, shiny black hair, perfect bangs framed large brown eyes outlined with black liner. The deep-red lipstick on her lips should have looked overdone against her pale skin, but it was the entire package that worked. She was as sexy as she appeared wholesome. Speechless, he took her in from the tips of the ballet flats she wore, up legs as long as a summer day, up the nip at her waist where the red and white gingham blouse had been belted. Bangle bracelets at her wrists. She was an ad for the updated, way sexier 1950s. It was all American but in that pinup sort of way. Vintage sexy and he really wanted some more.

And he'd seen her naked more times than he could remember. Which was a lie. He remembered every single time he'd been with Lily Travis naked.

"Um." He cleared his throat and loosened his tie. "Lily?" She'd not been this va-va-voom when they'd been in school. This was a woman who had a point of view. She'd grown up. This woman appeared to fully own the depth of her sexuality in a way she'd only begun to realize when they'd been together before. This personal style suited her very well.

She straightened and took a deep breath. The buttons at her cleavage did their work—barely—as her breasts thrust forward, stretching the material. His cock must have felt sympathy and that was why it stretched the material at his lap.

He searched for his words as he took her in. "Lily?"

She stepped into his classroom, and he couldn't seem to think of anything else to say as he watched the woman he'd once loved walk toward his desk. She still moved as if music played in her head.

His sister Beth was close to Lily so he knew she had been around more to deal with her little brother. But it hadn't prepared him for the punch to the gut at the sight of her.

"Mr. Murphy." She nodded once, all business. "I'm here about Chris. Do you have a few moments?"

"Chris?" He wondered if she wore stockings with garter belts and corsets. And then of course he had to imagine her dressed like that, because...well why not?

She sighed. "Chris Travis? Tenth grader? Hair too long? Surly? Problems with authority in all forms? He's failing your English class." She put the academic warning letter on his desk.

Oh, yes, that. "I can't really talk with you about this. I'm sorry. Your mother needs to do it. Or your father."

She pulled out yet another piece of paper to hand his way. "This is the paper that establishes my guardianship of my brother. My parents have signed the appropriate paperwork. It's all in order."

Reading through the paperwork to be sure everything was correct, he looked back to Lily. "All right then. I have about twenty minutes before my next class. Sit down and we can talk."

She did and he tried to pretend she was just another parent. And failed.

Her scent teased the air between them. Sultry and sexy. Like her voice. Full-on velvet, a throaty sort of purr that had always sent his brain, and other parts of his body, into overdrive. Still did.

Focus. "He's got a twenty percent in my class. He's here, at best, two days a week. Hasn't turned in an assignment in about six weeks. Even before that his work was sloppy and erratic."

Her shoulders slumped just a little, but he had to hand it to her, she straightened quickly enough. She took some notes, her little black glasses perched on her nose. Her nails were glossy red. The same red he'd be willing to bet she had on her toes.

She broke into his musings with a sigh. "So give me your honest opinion. Is this salvageable? Can he make this up or not?"

"He has to come to class, Lily. His absenteeism is the biggest problem. If he's not here when I cover the material, how can he learn it? He's just not here. The assignments he does finish tell me he gets what he's here for, though it's nearly impossible to give him full credit because I can't read the work. His writing is atrocious. He can do better."

"He'll be here. Every. Day."

Nathan didn't express his doubt in the statement. She seemed pretty driven to make it true, but trying to get a fifteen-year-old boy to do what he didn't want to do was a lot harder than she probably thought.

"Gonna take more than a phone call from another city to get that done." Why he poked at her he didn't know. But the flash in her gaze thrilled him.

She narrowed her eyes at him and sniffed as if he wasn't worth slapping. "Really? Oh gee, my plan has been foiled already." She sent him a raised brow and he barely held back a laugh. "I moved back to Petal. I'm living with my mother and Chris. I'm bringing him to school in the morning and picking him up in the afternoons. *I'm here* for the long haul. I want Chris to succeed, and *I'm here* to see how I can do that with the help of his teachers."

Oh. Well then. This was something he'd have to do very carefully, but if she was back, he'd have the chance to make things up to her. Maybe they could see what dating would be like as adults instead of kids in college. Not if she had someone though. Her ring finger was bare, which was a good sign.

"Must have sucked to move away from your life in Macon." The moment he finished speaking he wished he could have sounded a little more natural and a little less forced casual.

Lily tapped her pen and neatly avoided his statement. Did he think she would just pretend nothing had ever happened between them? She was prepared to do that, but only if she never actually had contact with him. Which given her current circumstance would prove difficult.

This was the first time she'd spoken to him since that night. Nausea roiled through her belly as she remembered walking into the living room at a party he'd been at and found him kissing another woman.

Remembering that and the way she'd felt afterward was enough to get rid of that damned tingle he gave her and a reminder that he was a tool.

While she gave him her best look of total disdain, she noted he'd grown even more handsome than he'd been before. Not just handsome, but that sort of gorgeous a southern girl like herself was absolutely helpless against. Hell, any woman anywhere.

Nathan Murphy was all southern honey. He had that slow, sexy delivery. His voice had the right amount of smoke, always the hint of a smile. That sound that'd been, and most likely still was, a magnet to underpants all across Georgia. He moved that way too, took his time to look around. Always late but he was so charming he got away with it.

A cruel twist of fate that he'd turned out so well. It was small of her, but she'd wished him a potbelly and male pattern baldness a few times. And here he was looking mighty fine. She hadn't had sex or even a boyfriend in about a year. He caught her at an already weak moment, and no matter how many lectures she'd given herself in the hallway outside, it *did* matter that she'd loved him once. It mattered that he'd walked away from it and never appeared to even care.

Still, mmm, that thick head of hair looked soft. She knew what it felt like against the skin of her inner thighs, in her hands as she sat behind him in his big old bathtub and washed it. Caramel. It was the color of burnt sugar, and it matched the well-defined beard and mustache he had now. His shoulders were still powerful as the muscles showed against his shirt when he turned to grab something out of his top drawer.

He kept talking like she wasn't imagining him naked. "He's pretty far gone. But here are some extra-credit assignments. I want all four of them done and I want quality work. I won't be doing him any favors if I let him slide."

Did she ask for that? Good gracious. But, he was in charge and her brother had messed up so it was time to suck it up and deal. She nodded, taking the papers and reading them over. "All right. He'll do them."

"I know things have been hard since..."

No. Not there and not with him. "He always was a crappy father. Chris can't let our father hurt him any more than he already has. It's not going to bring him back if Chris has to take summer classes or fail tenth grade. I'm not here to make excuses for him. He knows he's been slacking and he knows I aim to make him stop."

He paused, licking his lips before he spoke again and little tingles spread out from all her best places. "Your momma's okay with this?"

"I know she's been a problem." Which had been such a lovely thing when she'd lived far enough away, not to be drawn into her mother's passive aggressive ways of getting attention. The drinking only made it worse. "Which is why I have the guardianship. She's been too lenient to try to make up for our father leaving. Chris knows how to work her and get what he wants. But I'm not her."

Thank God. If she had been, maybe Lily never would have had the nerve to box up Nathan's stuff and leave it on his doorstep along with a check to cover his half of the security deposit on the apartment they'd rented together. It wasn't the way he'd kissed Alison. Her *cousin* Alison. Lily knew her cousin had been throwing herself at Nathan in the time he and Lily had been taking some space from one another. It was the way he'd made her feel when he never bothered to try to talk to her about it.

Gah! Enough. Back to Chris and the situation with her mother.

It wasn't that Pamela didn't care about her children. It was that she often found it best to get attention by letting Nancy show up and complain and criticize while Lily tried to ignore it. That way drama swirled all around and their mother got to be part of it without being a target.

As their mother never did a thing to stop it, Lily had learned over her life that the best way to deal with her sister was not to let her ruffle feathers. Lily just pretended Nancy wasn't standing there carping about something she was far too lazy to have done herself.

The only balancing act would be to keep their mother from getting drawn into it for entertainment. The last thing Lily wanted to do was mother her own darned parent, but it appeared to be what was needed. Because it was Chris who mattered right then. Not Nathan Murphy looking all handsome and smoking hot or anyone else. Lily knew she was the only one in Chris's life who could make a difference, and she meant to do it. Whether he liked it or not.

Nathan looked back to the papers on his desk and then to her again. "He's also missing assignments. I want them all completed and turned in. You can go online to see exactly what he's missing. The school has a link on the website. I have a mini-site too with all assignments and directions available. If you have any questions, just ask."

She wrote more down. Having all the stuff available online would help her a lot because she knew she couldn't trust Chris to keep her updated.

"All right, thank you. He'll get it done."

He hesitated. "Lil...Lily, some of the kids he's hanging out with aren't going to give you any help in getting Chris turned around."

He told her a few names and she thanked him, standing and tucking her things in her bag. She needed to go. Be away from Nathan who made such an attractive target for her attentions right then. Like that can of Pringles, he had to be resisted because he was bad for her.

She needed to keep him squarely in the authority-figure camp. He was her brother's teacher. She was resourceful and intelligent, she could overrule her ovaries and get the job done. Pull up her big-girl panties and all those sayings. Forever and ever, amen.

She withheld her sigh at the discovery that in his presence her ovaries had the wheel and they were *not* letting go.

"Would it be all right if I checked in with you every few days to make sure he's doing what he should be?"

19

He stood and moved toward her so she scooted toward the door. "Yes, of course." He handed her a card. "My email and numbers are there. I check email each morning, at noon and then at four or so. If I can count on you and we can work together, we might be able to get Chris to his junior year."

"Thank you. I mean that."

"Why don't we catch up over pie and coffee later?"

"No thank you, I'm busy." She was very proud of the way she'd managed to sound as if she didn't care at all.

"We used to be friends, remember?" He stepped closer and made her dizzy.

"I'm *friends* with your sister. I have enough friends."

Beth Murphy was one of her best girlfriends. Growing up, Beth had practically lived at her house every summer, and given the situation the Murphy kids had at home, neither of her parents had ever complained to see Beth sleeping over.

But then Lily had gone to college and ended up with Nathan. It had been like a fairy tale at first. He was the handsome boy from back home. Older. Sophisticated. And really hot. Plus he taught her plenty of sex-type stuff that unfortunately she'd never found a man good enough to replicate. She'd considered him The One. It was fabulous until it all fell to pieces.

She and Beth had remained good friends, but they'd grown apart a little, especially after the breakup and then when she'd moved to Macon. As friends went, Lily considered herself to be very fortunate to have one in Beth, and it was one of the things she considered best about moving back to Petal.

Now for the thing she dreaded most about moving back to Petal. She sighed as she hiked her bag up to her shoulder.

"Thanks for the help." She opened the door and nudged

him aside to get past. He was solid and warm and still smelled really good. And she was totally sure he'd meant to brush against her the way he had. Man he was sneaky.

She'd once loved him more than anything or anyone in the world. Times change.

So close to her just then he caught sight of the flutter of her pulse at the hollow of her throat and the scent of her perfume wafted over. He imagined her body heating for him, the way his was for her. Her lips parted just a breath and he caught his own but drew her into his lungs and the shock of it echoed through his gut.

Ensnared, he drew another deep breath and barely managed to keep from burying his face in her hair. "You still wear frangipani?" He couldn't help but smile. He loved the earthy scent she wore. He wanted to ask if she still put it behind her knees and in the hollow of her throat. But the look on her face told him that would be a bad idea.

But he was hungry for her. A hunger he hadn't admitted to himself in a really long time. But there she stood, close enough to touch and he couldn't.

And he had no one to blame but himself.

Chapter Two

Lily walked out to her car after six meetings with six teachers. A whole rasher of begging and apologizing and a lot of promises had been given. The principal liked Chris and believed in him, which was a huge help.

But the state was already giving them the evil eye about all the absences, and Lily had to sign an official warning saying that if he continued to cut class, he'd be expelled and have to be home schooled and they'd have to deal with child-protective services too.

That was the last thing any of them needed. The general store on Main should carry some of the organizational supplies she'd need for his room. A trip to Atlanta or one of the bigger towns closer in would be necessary to get the rest. Or she could order off the internet.

Seeing the Honey Bear, she pulled in and parked. Once she'd grabbed some carbs, she decided to hit the bookstore to see if they carried any of the books Nathan had listed for his extra-credit assignments.

They did and they had some calendar stuff she needed as well.

"Hi there. Wow! You look fabulous."

Lily turned to see the freaking fashion model behind the counter holding a toddler with pale blonde hair and big green eyes to complement her wicked grin. That was new. Not babies, but the woman wasn't someone she recognized.

"Um, thanks."

Glamazon smiled, looking even prettier. "I'm Cassie and this is Meg, my niece." A greedy little hand plopped a big plastic horse on the counter and soon, another set of big green eyes and a mop of dark brown hair showed themselves. She laughed. "Not a daycare, I promise. That's Ward, my son. Sorry, my sister-in-law ran to grab some lunch. You new around here?"

"No, actually. I grew up in Petal. I'm Lily Travis. Just moved back. This week in fact. Is Penny around?"

"She sold the store to me a few years back. She's married now, with two kids. Lives in Atlanta. Lily? You and Beth Murphy are friends, right? Your mom is Pamela Travis?" The brief look that flashed across Cassie's features told Lily the entire town knew about her father.

"I've known Beth since first grade. I've liked her since third." Lily laughed. "And yep, Pamela is my mother. You're not from around here. I'd remember that hair."

Cassie laughed, and the little girl she held laughed and clapped as well.

"Thank you. Not originally. I didn't plan to end up here. But a few minutes after I drove into town, I was rear-ended by the woman who turned out to be my future mother-in-law. I was a goner when I saw all eleven feet of handsome gorgeous that was her son. Oh and look, it's my sister-in-law. Well, more than one of them."

Lily turned to see a petite blonde with a baby so clearly her own in one of those baby-carrier things women wore, her hands full of bags. Next to her a sleek-looking, visibly pregnant brunette holding the hand of a preschooler.

Suddenly the place was awash with Chase wives. Lily smiled at the blonde. "Hey you."

Tate Murphy, or rather, given the pictures her mother had taken at her wedding reception, Tate Chase, hugged her around

23

the baby in the sling. "Oh my God! Lily! You're here. Beth said you'd be in town a bit."

"You look fabulous." She looked her friend over after they broke the hug. "Marriage suits you. Then again, if I was married to Matt Chase, I'd look satisfied and a little bit smug about it too."

Tate grinned. "I have a very good life and that includes a pretty tasty-looking man to come home to every night. It's good to see you. Olivia? You remember Lily?"

Lily looked around Tate and smiled at the woman she remembered from back in the day. "Marc Chase I hear. My mom keeps me apprised of all the comings and goings. Congratulations to you too."

"You were a few grades down from me. I was in Nancy's class."

Olivia sent a raised brow to Tate, who laughed. "It's okay, Lily knows what her sister is." Tate turned back to Lily as they moved to put all the bags of food on the counter. "Give me an update. What's going on with things?"

She told them a little, just the basics. If Nathan was still close to his sister—and she knew he would be—he'd tell her himself. He valued family; it was one of the things she'd admired about him, and he and Tate were especially tight.

"Well, I'm glad to have you back." Tate held the curve of the baby in the sling as she leaned down to kiss the toddler in Cassie's arms. "Beth's been so happy to have you around. I'm glad you're back for good."

"I need to call her. I've been meaning to, but things keep getting in the way. I haven't spoken to her in a week."

"She'll understand. Sounds like you've had a lot to do."

"Yeah. Speaking of that, I have to get going. I need to pick

Chris up from school and I want to drop some stuff off first. Cassie, it was nice meeting you. Nice seeing you again, Liv. Tate, when you see Beth, please tell her I'll be calling." She paid for the books and said her goodbyes once more before heading out to her car.

"Lily."

She looked up to see Tate coming out of the store.

"Nathan would like to see you too, I'm sure."

"I've been over to the high school already. He's one of Chris's teachers."

"He's single."

"Not surprised. But it has nothing to do with me."

"I know he did you wrong. *He* knows he did you wrong. But you two were good together."

It was impossible not to love Tate Chase. "Subtlety is not your strong point."

Tate laughed and hugged Lily again. "I fully expect you to be at Shane and Cassie's house for Martini Friday. All my sisters will be there. All the Chase wives. We've got a great group of friends and I know you'd fit in like you never left."

She paused. It had been hard...after the breakup. She'd had to distance herself from the Murphys and it had felt as if she lost part of her family. They hadn't made her feel bad or anything, but just being around them made her think of Nathan and she couldn't do it. It would be a good thing to have a group of close women friends again. "All right. Thank you for asking."

Tate scribbled down an address and handed it back.

The baby in the carrier squealed and kicked her legs. Her smile was as easy and charming as Matt's had been back in the day.

"You and Matt sure do make some sweet kids."

25

"This is Elizabeth, but we call her Lil Beth. She's pretty much all about her daddy except when she's hungry."

"Can't blame her. She's clearly got good taste."

Tate's already wide smile brightened. "I'm glad you're back, Lily. I've missed having you around."

Maybe, just maybe—she mused as she drove slowly through town, calling out her hellos through the open windows—she missed being around too.

Nathan walked into his sister's house and grinned at the sight. He didn't bother knocking or using the bell. No one would have heard it anyway.

This was his life. Filled with all these people he loved. Not a bad way to end a day.

Tate and Matt's house was the chief gathering place for the Murphy siblings. Wall-to-wall adults, kids out in the spacious backyard playing and running. It was normal. Nice and normal. And totally noisy.

Nathan and his siblings didn't have much normal when they were growing up in that tiny, suffocating trailer. But Tate had raised them, had given them all as much love as they'd needed and more. And now she was an amazing mother to her two children and her husband adored her. No one deserved it more.

Tate returned his smile when she looked up, waving him toward the kitchen where she stirred a series of pots on the stove. "Nathan Murphy! You're late."

"Hi there, hon." He bent to kiss the top of her head. "Sorry. I have a problem kid in my class and I met with his sister today. I wanted to check in with some of his other teachers."

"You didn't miss anything. Other than mentioning the problem kid's sister was none other than Lily Travis." She paused, turning her head. "Meg! You give that back to Lise right now."

He laughed at his niece, who gaped at her mother's seemingly superhuman ability to know exactly when she was up to trouble. "Deal with it, kiddo. She has eyes in the back of her head."

Her brow furrowed, just like her mother's did. "Daddy!" she howled as she tore out of the room.

"Always runs to daddy." Tate snorted.

"Matt's a smart guy, not like he's going to overrule you."

Tate grinned. "Well, he's smitten with all the women in his life."

"Where's the littlest of his women anyway?" He looked toward the swing, which was empty, and the little saucer thing Lil Beth jumped in and spun around while squealing.

"Matt's doing a diaper check. So back to the subject. I ran into the most gorgeous woman today in Cassie's bookstore. Like she stepped out of a magazine ad from 1958. Cute pants and shirt. Matching jewelry. Really just a whole package."

He groaned. "Chris is in trouble. She's come back to Petal to straighten him out. He needs it, Lord knows. But she's got a big job ahead of her. I don't envy it."

Tate harrumphed. "Are we pretending you don't care that she's back in Petal?"

He put his hands up defensively. "She's the one who dumped me. This is strictly professional. You know I'm not looking for anyone right now." Not after his last girlfriend had gotten though with him and his bank account.

"Oh fuck that fucking woman! That's what you get for

27

trusting a grown person who wanted people to call her Steffie. I told you she was trouble." Tate hissed angrily as she looked around to be sure no kids were nearby.

"I thought you were working on your little F-word issue." He hid a smile. His beautiful, petite sister had a mouth a sailor could envy.

"I am! I was. But she makes me want to say all the really bad words and there aren't any kids around to hear and so I stumbled a little." She managed to make her sniff sound indignant, and Nathan only loved his sister more for it.

She shot a glare his way again briefly before turning her attention back to meal prep. "Stephanie needs her butt kicked to Texas and back. But you're just as dumb. She was a skank, much like the rest of them have been. Which is why Lily dumped you, dumbass."

"I clearly need to stop making any commitments to women I'm not related to. I'm not cut out for long-term relationships." He shrugged, wishing he felt what he was saying. But with Lily back in Petal, it seemed a thinner excuse than it had been even a few days before.

The vegetables she was chopping shook a little from the force she was putting into it for a few breaths. "Oh you *clearly* need to stop making commitments? What commitments would those be? Aside from your *lack* of commitments to anyone since her, your real problem is that you've got appalling taste in women. Other than Lily Travis that is. You ignore all the suitable women you come across to focus on one pretty and totally vicious woman after the next. You can't commit to that and thank God you don't."

"The one time I go for a woman like Lily and look how it turned out. Exactly the way it does with the rest."

"Do you really expect me to believe you care as little for Lily breaking things off with you as you did when Stephanie did? Really? I call poop on that," she corrected with an eye toward the dining room.

He squirmed a bit, knowing she saw right through him. "She's a good person. I'd like to be friends with her again. But the last thing I need is to go sniffing around after anything more than that. She's back in Petal to help with Chris but what about when he straightens up? She'll head out to Macon and her old life."

"You're lots of things, Nathan, but a quitter isn't one of them. You're the smart one in the family. Act like it." She *hmpf*ed and he laughed.

The only woman he'd ever been able to count on stood right there in that kitchen. Lily had been the glaring exception in what had been his choice of women for romance. He had horrible taste. He was a menace to himself.

"What can I do to help?" He picked up a bowl of green beans.

"You think I'm letting you change the subject, Nathan, but I'm not. Lily is good for you and she's back. I can't for the life of me imagine why you'd let her go the second time. You're pretty, but you're not dumb. Now, take those beans out and get the garlic bread from the oven. We'll start dishing up the food for the kids before calling them in."

He nearly kicked the tile floor and said, "Aww, Tate!" but his pride kept his control.

She took his arm after he'd called the kids in from outside. "All that nameless, faceless fuckbuddy business is beneath you, Nathan. You need a woman who's worthy of you. Stop dragging the bottom of the barrel and you might find one who won't screw you over. Lily loved you something fierce. She's exactly the kind of woman you need. You made a mistake, but I believe you two have been given another chance. Don't mess it up this time."

She tiptoed up, kissed his cheek and swatted his behind with a towel as she guided the kids who'd just started to come in the door to their seats.

And he thought about what his world would be like with Lily in it and then realized he didn't know. He'd certainly changed in the last six years, she would have too.

But it wasn't an altogether bad thing. He realized he really wanted to find out who they were after all this time.

"Lily, where are the keys to my car?" Pamela wandered into the room.

Lily looked up from the essay she was proofing for her brother. "On the counter. Why? Do you need me to run an errand for you?" There was no way she was letting her mother drive in the state she was in.

"Chris needs to run to a friend's house. He needs to borrow it."

She looked at her mother, blinking. "We talked about this."

"He told me he made it through the whole week without being late once."

"It's *one* week. He hasn't turned in an assignment in his math class since November. He's on lockdown, Mom. He's got a long way to go to keep from failing his entire sophomore year."

"Nancy thinks you should give him some rewards."

She looked around the room. "Nancy's not here. I am. Now, I told him no and you said you'd back me up. Worse, he *knows* he's not allowed to have the car."

"I'm his mother, Lily. It's my job to take care of him."

She looked at her mother and held back the scream of frustration roiling in her gut. She wanted to yell, *So do it!* But it wouldn't help to get angry. Pamela would retreat and it would only complicate matters with Chris.

But.

"I didn't give up my house and my life in another city to move here and help with Chris, to be undermined at every step. We made a plan. The counselor seems to think it's a good plan. He's responding really well to our united front. And to the stability. He's going to school and turning his work in. Now he has to clear out the backlog. As for these friends of his, you and I both know none of them are good for him. We agreed to hold him accountable. Period. He needs stability. We need to stay strong. This is for him and his benefit."

Pamela sighed, but Lily could see her spine hunch a little as she let it go.

Lily stood. "I'll handle Chris myself." She'd been the one to deal with the homework anyway.

He had the good sense to show fear in his eyes when she came into his room. "Expecting to see Mom instead?" She tossed the paper to him. "Took the liberty of helping you recognize your potential. That's sloppy work and you're capable of more."

"I'll do it better next time."

"Oh I'm sure you will. And you'll do better this time too. Right now. You have time since you won't be going anywhere. Don't go around me to her again."

He stuck his chin out, defiant. "She's my mother."

"She's mine too. And we both know she's having a rough time of it right now. So I'm in charge. It's not ideal, but it's what you've got. Get your act together and stop being a brat. Everyone's too tired for it." She waved over her shoulder as she left the room. "Bring me the revisions. I'm going up to my room now."

Chapter Three

Lily wasn't sure why she was nervous. After all, she'd known Beth Murphy most of her life and through her, Beth's sisters. She knew Maggie Chase and probably every woman on the other side of the door.

She knocked before she could change her mind only to have the door yanked open by a grinning Beth Murphy. "Sugar, you're here!"

She hugged her friend and was yanked inside.

Maggie Chase approached, grinning. "It's been way too long since I've seen you last. Come on in."

Lily put her bag on the little bench at the entry and kicked off her shoes, following Maggie and Beth into the wide and full living room.

"We've got sour apple and lemon drops made so far. Want one?" Beth indicated the counter lined with pretty martini glasses and two pitchers.

A lemon drop in her left hand, she managed to nod a lot at the stuff people said as she made her way to the couch to sit.

"You know everyone, right?" Beth asked.

"Let's see." She looked around. "Yep. I met Cassie a few days ago at the bookstore. I know everyone else from school or town."

Beth hugged her side. "I've missed you so much. I've hated living in two different places. And when you come back to visit, it's..."

"Awkward. It's all right. It put you in an odd spot and I didn't want to make things worse after we broke things off. But I've missed you too."

"You're back for good, right?" Maggie passed over a tray of something yummy looking so Lily took two. Just to be neighborly and all.

"I had thought it would be temporary, but Chris is going to need me. He's too much for my mom and he's nervous enough about people leaving him. I made a promise that I'd be here for him and I will."

Tate smiled, nodding. "Nathan says he's seeing a big difference since you've been back. It's good you can do it. I know he'll appreciate it in the end."

"Not so much when I take his car away and he starts with how I'm not his mother." She laughed and raised her glass.

Tate laughed. "Chris will take a while. But I think your being here for him is exactly what he needs."

"What's your job situation?" Beth snuck one more of the little meatball things off the tray and winked at Lily.

"I can do my job remotely. For a while anyway. Eventually they're going to want someone based in Macon, and I get that. Once upon a time I made an okay living with my freelance work. I don't know if that's the case anymore. But I have some other ideas as to how I can pay the rent."

"You're living with your mom?"

"Above the garage, which is the same really. But it's close enough, and I can be around to make sure Chris gets to school and that he's not sneaking around and cutting class. My mom is... Well I'm glad I'm nearby."

"I was sorry to hear about what your dad did. How is she recovering from that? How are you?" Beth's voice was low enough that it wasn't a loud public statement. Conversation picked up all around them and Lily let herself relax.

"He didn't cheat on me and drop our marriage and child for some twenty-year-old. What I have to deal with is nothing compared to that. At the same time, this isn't his first trip to another woman's bed. I know it makes me uncharitable, but he's always been the center of the universe and everyone was supposed to be a satellite around him. My mother made that choice to live that way. I didn't. So she's a wreck. I hope she snaps out of it and can be a better and more present mother for Chris, but I don't know if it'll happen. I sure know Chris doesn't have the time to wait around for it or for our father to get his head out of his rear and remember he's got other things in addition to his too-young girlfriend to support."

"Well, you know my history. If you want to talk about it, I'm around. I love your mom, but even I can see she's sort of given up."

Beth's parents were far worse than Lily's ever could have been. For her, it had been neglect, but mainly benign. The Murphy parents were a living nightmare.

"Nancy has been sniffing around."

Beth made a sour face. "You need another drink for that, and then you and I are going to talk about Nathan."

Lily put her hands over her face, but laughed anyway.

"What? What are you embarrassing her over? You have to share so we can snicker too." Cassie leaned in, smiling.

"Nathan and Lily used to be together back in college."

"*Seven* years ago. It was nearly seven years ago." Her face blazed.

"Ha. Clearly you've forgotten all about it since you know exactly how long ago it was." Beth handed her another drink.

"And you need to try those little popover things there." She pointed to another plate.

"What'd he do?" Cassie asked. "What?" She looked around, laughing. "You all might know but I don't. I wager most of you don't know and want to know, but you're all just too chicken to ask. I'm a Northerner so I get to be rude. Polly told me that last week and I'm clutching it close as an excuse now. Don't be jealous. I'll share."

Lily winked. "I surely do like you, Cassie Chase."

"Okay, hang on. Let's top off everyone's drinks and bring out the rest of the food before we go into the story." Maggie went to grab some more plates of food, Olivia moving to join her.

"It's not even a big deal. We were both young. He's moved on. I moved on."

Beth rolled her eyes. "He's been agitated since Monday. Don't tell me he's moved on."

"I heard he was engaged. Sounds like it to me. And to Stephanie Prater?" She hated Steffie. She'd been a stupid, shallow girl in school, and Lily had no doubt was still stupid and shallow. Just the idea that Nathan considered *her* worth marrying and Lily not even worth explaining to made her want to punch something.

Tate laughed. "To a grown woman who made people call her Steffie. She showed up to his house with wedding invitations made!"

"Sad she has self-esteem issues."

"You are such a good addition to this group." Olivia put her feet up and sipped her virgin drink. "Marc and Nathan are a lot alike. All those pretty men with ladies falling over their feet to get to them, and they get lazy. You take work I bet. And I mean that as a compliment."

"Well I certainly require that any man I date who says he loves me doesn't go kissing up on other women."

"He did not!" Anne's eyes widened. Anne was another one of Nathan's sisters and also part owner of Tate's salon. "He's always been so closed mouthed about it. I guess I know why now."

"He did. But we were on a break so whatever. He never found it very important to try to explain and that is that. Period. I'm either worth it, or I'm not."

"I didn't know he never tried to explain and I sure never knew he cheated." Anne frowned. "I need to thump him."

"Please don't. Really." Why it was important to her that his family not be angry with him, she didn't know, but it was. "We were on a break, but we'd promised to not see anyone else while we worked things out. He apparently found his answers and acted on them before talking to me. We were young. I was twenty-one years old! I didn't know anything about anything, but I do know despite his flaws when it comes to women, Nathan is a good person. Please don't be mad. I shouldn't have said anything."

Beth patted her knee. "Don't worry. We all still love him. I find it interesting you're concerned over how we think about Nathan. Are you going to protect his virtue? 'Cause that's a big job."

Tate snorted. "And he saw the light with Steffie and broke things off. She's crazy too. Oh girl, she shows up all over town and scares him."

Ha! Good.

"Yes, I smirk a little too. Still, he's not the same selfish boy he was when you two were together before." It seemed a nice punishment that Tate would smirk over something Nathan did.

Lily put her hand up. "Enough talk about Nathan Murphy.

37

He moved on. I moved on. It was a silly romance years ago. Loving someone more than they love you is a sucky thing. But I'm over it."

They let the topic pass and moved on to other things. Gossip was pretty much the same as it had been when she lived there before. But when she got home later that night and had checked in on Chris, she realized it'd been the right choice to go. The right choice to start building a life here in Petal, for the long haul.

Her condo in Macon was up for sale. She just had to hope that despite the economy she could move it soon enough. Then she'd have a good down payment for her own place in town. It'd go some way in convincing Chris she had no plans to leave. And it'd give her a sense that she was putting down roots.

She was approaching thirty and it was time to settle in for real.

"I can't believe I let you talk me into this." Lily followed Beth through the crowd toward the table of women near the dance floor.

"You don't let anyone talk you into anything. You have a strong will, Lily Travis. You wanted to come here to kick up your heels and dance. Takes the edge off a crappy week." Beth grabbed her hand and tugged her along. Murphys never seemed to move slowly—except for the one.

At the thought of Nathan, she drew a deep breath and made herself think about Josh Lucas instead. Which worked for five seconds.

Tate, Anne and Maggie Chase waved them over when they caught sight of their approach.

"Hey you two. Pitcher just arrived. I heard about how you chased your brother and caught him by jumping a fence." Tate pushed a beer in Lily's direction. "That's awesome. Once when Jake was in trouble for something or other, can't remember what now, Tim jumped the fence at the drive-in and caught him." Everyone laughed, imagining the look on Jacob's face as his six-foot-plus brother cleared something so tall and then got close enough to grab.

"The boy will be the death of me." She gulped the beer as she watched the ebb and flow of people on the dance floor. "I can't believe the little shit made me chase him in the first place. I didn't think about it until I was nearly up and over it. Lucky I didn't land on my ass and break something."

"Was he with other kids?"

"Yes. I grabbed one of them too and marched him home. Chris told me he got put on restriction for six months. At least he got in trouble, I guess. The other two are little thugs and I've forbidden Chris from hanging with them. Who knows if it'll take or not. I'm now the meanest sister in the world." She mock bowed.

Beth snorted. "I bet Chris is good and scared of you now, though."

"He does jump every time I walk into a room." She raised her glass to the group. "Why are we here? I thought we'd head to Riverton."

"Used to. But the Tonk is closer." Beth shrugged. "It's sort of become our place over the last few years."

"How's your momma?" Maggie asked. "Polly saw her on Wednesday out in the yard. She been sick? Polly said she seemed pale."

That was the million-dollar question, wasn't it? Her mother had taken to drinking along with the pills and walked around the house in a daze. Lily hated for Chris to see it. If it went on much longer, she'd have to deal with it, and there was already so much to deal with, Lily wasn't sure she could do it all. Much less do it all right.

So she sighed. "She's a mess. But she stays out of my way when I'm dealing with Chris for the most part, so that's good. I guess."

She and Beth had talked about it, about this growing addiction. Beth and her siblings knew what it was like to grow up in a house with addicts. It wasn't pretty and Beth had a very low tolerance for it. Lily got that. It was bad for Chris to see, though she wasn't sure he got it quite yet.

"If you need anything, let me know." Tate reached out to squeeze her hand. "I understand more than you think."

She was wrong there, of course. Lily knew exactly how hard Tate had worked to raise her siblings around the violent, drunken episodes between her parents, and the ones her father had aimed at the children who were clearly not his own. She'd seen firsthand what Tate's face had looked like after she'd jumped in-between Beth and their father, and he'd taken out all that anger on her.

"I appreciate that." But damn it she didn't want to think on it. Wanted a few hours of some peace and lighthearted fun before she had to dive back in.

"Where is Chris tonight?" Beth passed the tray of potato skins over.

"Church youth group. Their youth pastor is a good guy. A few of Chris's friends are going. Friends he doesn't get in trouble with. Anyway, they're doing a sleepover in the rectory and watching movies. I don't want to take everything away from him. You know? I want him to have friends and a life. I just don't want that life to include having to jump fences to catch him when he's cutting school."

The subject was dropped after some laughs, and they got down to the business of ogling the denim butts on the dance floor. Not a whole lot she found sexier than a man in a cowboy hat, jeans and boots with a button-down shirt. Yum. Even better when they were all polite. She knew the Chase husbands lurked around at their own manly table elsewhere, but a girl can still look even if she's not gonna touch after all.

"Who is that?" Royal Watson, Anne's used-to-be-boyfriend now best friend, leaned over to ask Nathan.

He turned to find himself mesmerized by the sway of a spectacular pair of breasts that happened to belong to none other than Lily Travis.

"That is not yours. That's who she is." Nathan frowned as she took a circuit of the floor with Andy Sanchez. Andy's hand was mighty close to Lily's ass. That was not going to happen. It was one thing to know she was still pissed at him after all these years. He could live with that. Probably. But it was another to imagine her with anyone else in town. *That* wasn't going to be a reality he'd have to live with.

"Really now?" Royal grinned and looked pointedly at Nathan's hand. "Don't see any ring there. Why don't you...holy shit, that's Lily!" Royal found this ridiculously funny and Nathan wanted to punch him.

"Yes, it's Lily. Stop laughing."

"I laugh because your pain is amusing." Royal shrugged.

Matt Chase came back over. "Sorry, I had to go smooch up on my woman for a bit. She let me and then shooed me off. Don't know why we can't all sit together."

"Probably because Lily is with them and she hates Nathan."

"Thanks Royal, you can stop with that now before I have to clean your clock." Nathan watched her move, watched Andy lean in and say something in her ear. Watched her laugh and then thankfully shake her head and step back.

When she turned to head toward the women's table, her gaze snagged on his. He caught the awareness shocking through her system and sent her a smile. Oh, yes, he still got to her.

"I think you should ask her to dance." Matt hogged the nachos and Nathan frowned.

"I think he should too. Then she'll kick him in the stones, and we can laugh and laugh. Mr. Smooth can't get hisself a woman. Never thought I'd see that day." Royal smirked.

"Every time I'm with you for longer than three minutes I know why my sister dumped you." Nathan rolled his eyes.

"She dumped me because I asked her to marry me. *Three times.* And she said no each time. Picky women. This town grows 'em like peaches. Christ. If you don't ask Lily to dance, I will."

"No you won't. You and Anne aren't romantic anymore, but she sure as hell isn't going to be all right with you rubbing up on a close friend. Lily's like family so if you wouldn't rub up on Beth, you can't rub up on Lily either."

Royal frowned. "You made that up to keep me away."

"You'll never know for sure."

Matt laughed. "True. But he's right about one thing. You and Lily need a dance. But she's going to say no if you take her on directly-like. So wait until she's out there again and cut in. She's got good manners, she'll be too nice to snub you in public."

"You're a devious man. I like that about you."

So he bided his time until eventually she ended up out there again, and he headed out, careful to avoid the spot where Steffie was. She'd been less than thrilled when they broke the engagement off and continued to send him cow eyes when she wasn't plotting his death.

He tapped Phin on the shoulder and the man shot Nathan a look of annoyance, but he stepped back and Nathan smoothly took his place, getting a secure hold on that waist so she couldn't bolt.

They danced well together. Always had. He knew she loved it and he'd always loved to hold her as they did. Loved that any man in the place could look his fill but she was his. Christ he was dumb to have let her go.

"Well hello there, Lily." He sent her his most charming smile. She was not impressed and frowned back at him.

"Why are you doing this?"

"There's no reason we can't be friends. If I remember rightly, you like dancin'. So do I. Why not dance together? Unless, you know, I'm too much for you to handle, and you can't bear to be around me if we're not smooching. That's okay too, by the by."

"You're so full of yourself. Smooching? Seems to me you're just fine getting that whenever you want it."

He mimed pain, holding a hand over his heart. "I'm wounded."

"Not enough for my liking."

He laughed. "I'd forgotten how vicious you could be. I am sorry. It was shitty of me. But I'm older and wiser and more discriminating than I once was."

She rolled her eyes, and he had to close his eyes for a second as the scent of her perfume wrapped around his senses.

"Why the eye roll?" he asked when he'd gotten hold of himself once more.

"Discriminating? You not only put your dick in Stephanie, you were going to marry her. That is *not* exactly discriminating in my book."

"I'd say something like she's not all bad, but that's a lie. I sort of...anyway, she came to my house for dinner and she had a stack of wedding invitations she was trying to choose. She'd taken out an ad in the engagements section of the paper and put our picture in it. One of her friends took it at some party! Anyway, I went along with it for a while, but in the end, I couldn't keep lying to her about it and I couldn't talk myself into marriage to a woman who didn't make my heart beat faster unless it was from sick fear. Do you have someone? Back in Macon?"

"I did." The song was ending, and he knew she'd break for it once it was over.

"Did like how? Like you broke up a while ago or..."

She sighed. "I've been single a while. Not that it matters to you, Nathan Murphy."

"Let me buy you a drink."

"No."

"Why you gotta be so hard? We used to be friends. Before we had the other, we were friends. I miss that."

The song ended and she extricated herself. "I missed a lot of things for a long time. But I don't now." She turned her back on him and stalked back to the table where heads bent close, he knew asking her for details.

Then Steffie headed in his direction and he had to melt into the crowd to escape.

Chapter Four

Two weeks later, thoroughly angry, Lily drove through town until she found her quarry standing around the new convenience store a mile from the high school.

She whipped into a space and got out, heading straight for him. "In case you've forgotten, it's a school day."

He turned with a start and tried to act cool in front of his friends.

Taking her phone out, she videoed the little scene as she continued walking to them.

"You're missing third period. I'm sure it's an oversight. So get in the car and let's go."

"I was meaning to go."

"Yeah? Well it looks like you really meant to be a loser and cut school to me. Congratulations. Top marks on that one. This isn't a discussion. I am not seeking your input." She turned her glare to the malcontents her brother had taken up with. "Do your parents know you're also *late* to third period?"

"What's it to you?" one of them, Paulie, if she remembered right, said as he smoked.

"You're nothing to me actually. But he"—she grabbed Chris's hand—"is everything. So, I guess, to be blunt, what I mean is, will your parents care that y'all are here when you're supposed to be in school?"

Chris groaned. "Let's go."

"You don't have to go with her. What's she going to do,

carry you?" Paulie sneered and she pitied his parents.

"Knock it off, Paulie." There he was, the sweet kid she got to see a few times a day. The one she knew could make it if she pushed him. And she was going to, even if she had to pick him up and drag him.

He got in the car without another word.

"You know, Chris," she said, pulling out of the lot and heading toward the school, "I was in the middle of a piece when the school called me. I told you they would. This bullshit is beneath you. Those dipshits you hang out with are too."

"I just lost track of time."

She sighed. "Don't insult me. You can lie to your friends and even Mom, but don't waste my time. I love you, kid. I think you are worth the effort." She parked and got out, loving the look of panic on his face. "But we're on my time now and you've broken your word. You didn't lose track of time. You shouldn't even be off campus to start with."

"I just needed some caffeine. I'll bring soda tomorrow. You don't have to go in. I'm going. I promise." He scampered toward the front doors.

"Unfortunately I do. Because I can't trust you, and the state would frown on my kicking your ass. And, because the school has had it with you. Come on."

"Other moms don't use bad words around their kids," he muttered.

"You're fond of reminding me that I'm not your mother." She hauled the door open and waited. "Also, dude, if the worst thing you ever did was say some bad words, we'd be ahead of the game."

She signed him in at the front office and, to his horror, accompanied him to class where she sat in the back, ignored the curious looks and worked quietly while class went on.

By the time the bell rang, Chris seemed more than ready to get to his next class so she let him go without her escort, but she did watch to be sure he made it inside. She would laugh when she got into her car, but for that moment, it was enough to remember the horrified embarrassment on his face. If he was a smart kid, he'd not do it again. But if he did, she'd sit next to him.

"Hello there."

Oh that voice.

She had been avoiding him all she could. Which wasn't always easy because he had a way of turning up wherever she was.

Nothing to be done about that now. Though she wanted to turn and run, she faced him instead, catching Nathan Murphy standing in the doorway to his classroom. His unruly dark hair tousled around his face. A sinfully handsome face. Lush lips, an honest-to-God cleft in his chin, big hazel-brown eyes. He was tall and currently filling out black jeans, and a long-sleeved shirt hugged his upper body. Good grief he melted her butter.

Years later, she had more...developed sexual tastes, and still he did it for her. The teacher thing rang her bell like it was dinnertime, and even though she knew him, flaws and all, that click between them hadn't died. Thick enough that it took work to shake herself free. Familiar enough that she didn't entirely want to.

"Mr. Murphy."

He quirked up that very talented mouth. "Nice to see you backing up your word." He moved to her, and she felt that energy between them, warm and distracting.

She shrugged, and he thought, *of course she did.* She was precisely the kind of woman who kept her word.

Lauren Dane

"You received the first batch of his assignments?"

"I did. He and I talked about it yesterday. He told me he was nearly finished with the first extra-credit assignment too."

What a fucking delight it had been to hear the rumor about Chris's older sister sitting in on his class and to have it be true. To have her standing right there before him cool and collected, while still managing to look as if she was ready to slay dragons and kick ass on her brother's behalf. It was ridiculously hot.

That morning she wore a pretty sundress, navy blue with white polka dots. Her hair was away from her face, held back by a pretty flower clip just below her right ear. She looked effortlessly fashionable and definitely feminine.

She sped his pulse, hardened his cock and made him fist his hands to keep from touching what was once his.

"Okay then. Have a nice day." She spun, the hem of her skirt swaying in time with her ass as she walked away.

He followed her out. "I have a free period. You want to grab a cup of coffee with me?"

She paused at her car door. "No, Nathan, I don't."

"We used to be friends. I'd like that again."

He wanted *more* than that. Had accepted that he really wanted to kiss her again, wanted to taste her and feel her skin bare and warm, against his own. But they could start at friends.

"We used to be a lot of things. I'm not that girl anymore." She opened her car door and suppressed a growl of frustration. Even managed to stay casual.

"And I'm not that guy anymore. I'm sorry, Lily. I'm sorry for a lot of things."

She paused, emotion washing over her face for a brief moment and hope surged. It wasn't over. There was a chance to still make something with her if he handled it right.

"I don't have the time for any of this. I don't need your apology nearly seven years later."

He put a hand on her door. "Maybe I need to give you one."

She breathed out long and slow. "I hope it works out for you. Wish you'd felt that way when it meant something." She sent him a raised brow as she got into the car, yanking to get his hand loose, but not hard enough she would have harmed him if he hadn't let go.

Damn it all, the harder she tried to resist what they had, still, between them only made him hotter. There was something wrong with him.

"Goodbye, Nathan."

He stepped back and waved. "Be seeing you around, Ms. Travis."

He realized as she drove away just how much he wanted her. Thankfully, he had an entire team behind him who'd help. He'd known the Chases long enough to have heard how the entire family backed each one of their sons when they found the woman they wanted. He had seven brothers and sisters *and* the Chases too. She didn't stand a chance.

Grinning, he headed back into the school.

Not even a week later, Lily came back in from dropping Chris off at school and found her mother having a heated conversation with her father while Nancy looked on. The girlfriend was also there.

"I don't see why you can't just sell the house and give me half. It's my half, after all."

"I live here. Your son lives here! It's not bad enough that

you left the way you did? Not enough that you cleared out the bank accounts and stole the electronics in the house? Not bad enough you humiliated me for years and then you do this? You want to sell my home out from under me so you can buy more stuff for her? Get out, Rodger. I've had enough."

"You two can live in a condo. They're nice. You don't need this big house. Heck, we can take part of the money and send Chris to military school to straighten his ass out."

Nancy nodded. Uncharitably, Lily wondered if their father had promised her some money for helping.

"This house belonged to my grandparents. I'm not selling it so you can go to Mexico with your whore." Her words were slurred, but Lily was so relieved her mother was showing some spine that she didn't interrupt.

"You're holding things up to push our wedding back," the girlfriend whimpered. "You lost him. Just let it go! You don't need this place. We want to start a family and our place is too small for it."

At that, her mother burst into tears, and the girlfriend sent a smug look toward Lily.

"Enough. You." She pointed to the girlfriend. "It's not necessary for you to be here. This is my mother's house, and you've got no right to make her cry *again*."

"You'll not talk to my future wife that way," her father stuttered out.

"I'm sorry, it's just... I can't take you seriously when you're walking around with this baby on your arm. I have T-shirts older than she is. Your future wife? Really? You're here trying to push my mother out of the home she's lived in most of her life so you and your little friend can have more money. Money you're not even entitled to." Yes, she'd taken the opportunity to run her mother over to Edward Chase's office, and they'd declared the trust the house was in as valid. Rodger Travis had no right to it. Lily's great-grandmother hadn't ever liked Rodger, but she'd been close with Lily. She placed the house in a trust before she died, deeding it over to Lily when she turned twenty-five. The house was actually hers, though she had no immediate plans to claim it and undo the trust.

Still she had a rental agreement with her mother to keep them all covered in precisely this situation. Her father wasn't going to harm her mother, at least not on this one issue.

"Also, Georgia isn't a community property state. You aren't entitled to half of anything. She stayed home with your children, hosted dinners for your work people, essentially lived her entire life for you. You can't take her house and the law will say the same."

"You keep out of it. You're only stirring up problems. Your sister tells me what goes on here. I don't approve."

"You don't approve of what? Me stepping in and doing your job 'cause you can't keep your business in your drawers? Chris is your son, not that you act like it. If I hadn't have come back to help, he'd be still failing his classes. As for whatever Nancy says, she's not here unless it's to borrow money so what does she know anyway? If you don't approve of another person raising your child, you could do it yourself."

"You're my daughter. You will respect me."

She shook her head slowly, wondering at what point it was where she finally saw him for the soulless, selfish asshole he was. "You aren't owed respect, you earn it. Take your whore and get out. The house is in a trust. It's not community property. She's not selling it, even if she could. You'll just have to send teenage Barbie here out to get a job and learn to live on your retirement. You don't even respect yourself, why should I respect you? You crap all over your family and pretend to be moral? Get out."

"You can't tell me to get out."

"As it happens, I can. You want to beat up on defenseless women, you've got a young one right there. You want his kids? Good luck with that. I hope you can keep him interested long enough to make it happen. You need money, ask her parents. You went to high school with them anyway. Oh, wait, that was her grandparents."

Her mother snorted a laugh through the tears. "She's right. You need to leave, Rodger. Don't come in again without knocking."

"This is my house!"

"It isn't. You know it's not even in your name. There's a trust the house is held in. It's not Mom's. It's not yours either. Go back to Atlanta and get your own house in order. You're not selling this house and that's final."

"We'll just see what my lawyer thinks about that." He grabbed Barbie's hand and stormed out. Nancy sent a dirty look over her shoulder. ·

"You drive him away!"

"You're too old to have daddy issues. Hit the road, Nancy. You might miss the gravy train if you don't rush. Though, he's got a lot less than you calculated. You and the girlfriend. Ha."

She put an arm around her mother and steered her into the living room.

"Sit. Let me get you some tea."

Nancy scampered to catch up, screeching to their father to wait for her.

"I'm so embarrassed." Her mother took the tea.

"Why? He's the one who's done wrong here."

"I took a lot. Chris probably saw things he shouldn't have. I tell myself I should forgive your dad. That if I really loved him I would. He's the father of my children after all. I loved him a long time. Maybe I still do. What if I'm making a mistake?"

"It is entirely possible to forgive something, to truly let go and wish that person well while at the same time making sure they can never get close enough to harm you again. Forgiveness is a gift, but it doesn't need to make you stupid. I can't tell you how to live your life, but if a man makes you cry on a regular basis, I can't think you're meant to love that man anymore."

"I don't know that I'm strong enough for this."

Lily took her mother's hands. "Let me help you a little. You're stronger than you give yourself credit for."

Her mother nodded and mopped her tears up. Lily wished she believed the nod meant her mother would try harder, but feared it would only get worse.

"Fancy seeing you here."

Nathan barely held his smile back as he sauntered into the Honey Bear where Lily sat at a booth with a camera at her right hand and coffee at her left.

She looked up, smiled thinly and her attention shifted away just as quickly.

Gave him the time to send his brother William—a baker at the Honey Bear and the man who'd texted Nathan to say he should come on by the café to say hello to an old friend—a thankful tip of the chin.

His family had his back and they all loved Lily from when they were kids, so they were thrilled to help, and he was relieved to have it.

"This seat taken?" he asked as he took it anyway. She

frowned at him momentarily and looked back down at the photos. "What's that?"

"Work."

He grinned and sipped. "What brings you out so early on a Saturday?"

"Work." Less nonchalant and more annoyed. This pleased him for some sick reason.

"I had a run. Thanks for asking. After this I'm heading over to Tate and Matt's for a barbecue later today. I've promised to be quizmaster. Beth said she invited you."

She sighed and looked up, tapping her pen quickly. "Don't let me keep you."

"I like the glasses." Ignoring her weak attempt to shoo him away, he raised his coffee in her direction. "Sexy."

She tried not to smile, he saw her struggle and then she lost it, shaking her head. "She did invite me. I can't because I'm taking Chris with me to Macon later today. I have some things I need to deliver to work."

"He's been showing improvement, Lil. You're doing a good job."

"*Lily.* And thank you. I hope so. Christ, the boy is going to make me start attending high school with him at this rate."

He laughed. "He's not cutting third period anymore I'm told."

Snorting, she sipped her coffee. "For such a smart kid, he has no common sense at all. Drives me insane."

"None of them do. I see it all day long. But the ones who get support from family snap out of it. They go to college and get good jobs. Start families. All the things you want for him. And because you care enough to sit in his class with him until he gets the message, he'll make it too."

She gathered her things. "I hope so. I'm off. Have a good day with your family."

He would have offered to carry her things to her car, but she'd only say no and she didn't have much anyway. She'd spoken with him, and not entirely about Chris, so things were moving in a positive direction at least.

She paused at the front door, turning back to face him. "Thank you. For all you've been doing for Chris. It makes a difference. A big one."

He watched her leave. Loving those sexy little librarian glasses.

"She didn't throw her coffee in your face." William came out and dropped into the booth across from Nathan. "That's a start."

"Three weeks ago she would have left when I came in. Progress, bro, progress."

"They don't call you the bulldog for nothing." William smiled at him over the rim of his mug.

"Oh God, I'd forgotten about that." Tate started that one. When Nathan was a kid he'd scrapped when he needed something, worked and worked until he got it. She said he was like a bulldog when there was something he wanted.

And he wanted Lily.

William shrugged. "Big brothers never forget. Anyway, I'll see you over at Tate's later. I'm working here another hour or two and then I'll get home. Cindy will have eleven thousand things she wants me to do in the yard before we go."

Nathan adored William's wife. Especially the way she handled his brother and accepted the insanity that came with being a Murphy.

"Thanks for the tip on Lily. Why don't I stop over in a bit to help with the yard?"

"Damn, I'd have called you before today when she came in if I had any idea I'd be able to get some yard work out of you."

William walked him out.

"It's going to work. She already likes your family. We already like her. I've never known you not to get what you wanted."

Nathan scratched his chin a moment. "I hope so. I hate that it's my fault she doesn't trust me." Up until two weeks before, he'd only told Tate and Tim the specifics of what had happened. He hadn't been proud of it. And he really hadn't been happy when Anne and Beth had barged into his house early on a Saturday morning after they'd heard what he'd done the night before from Lily.

He'd been pissed she tattled until Beth smacked him upside the head and told him how the details had come out and that Lily had said he was a good man. And then his sisters had promised help on his plan to woo Lily back.

"It was years ago, Nate. A kiss. One. Not that you weren't an ass, you were. But you've grown up and so has she. Take it slow. There's no timer on it. Get to know her again and let her get to know you. She'll see." William clapped him on the back. "In the meantime, it's awfully amusing to see you have to work for a woman. I'll see you soon. Bring your gloves. I need to clear out some brush."

Nathan groaned. "Fine. Thanks for the advice."

Chapter Five

She pulled into the driveway too late to see Nancy's car already there. Damn and double damn. Thankfully it was during the day so Chris wasn't home. She had a hair appointment and she should have just gone straight there.

As if she were made of lead, she climbed out and went inside. It would be good to stand her ground from the start, but it was never fun to be around Nancy. Even when her sister was in a good mood, she was simply a vicious bitch. Self-centered. Lazy.

So it wasn't a surprise to find Nancy with her feet up, smoking a cigarette. As her mother clearly hadn't, Lily felt less than comfortable telling her sister to put it out. At the same time, one of the things Lily had just gotten under control was not only her own asthma but Chris's.

"Hey, Nancy. Didn't expect to see you here." Keep it civil and brief. Over the years, Lily knew the best way to deal with her sister was to not let herself be goaded into a fight over nothing.

"I bet. I was just telling Mom that if you lived with me you'd have to do a lot more for your rent."

But being civil didn't mean she'd line up to be abused either. "Oh, bless your heart, hon. Guess it's a good thing I'm here and not in your tiny little studio in Atlanta." She smiled calmly. "By the way, please don't smoke in the house. Chris's asthma is just barely under control again."

"I was saying the same thing." Pamela looked to Lily and for the first time, she saw relief there.

"You should have said." Nancy stabbed it out and turned her gaze back to Lily.

Before she could drag Lily into another verbal round of hurt your sister, Lily pulled her bag up on her shoulder, standing tall. "It was nice to see you, Nancy. Mom, I dropped off the stuff for the jumble sale. Merline says she'd sure love to see you on Saturday afternoons again."

Pamela brightened a little. Lily wanted to see it more. Wanted her mother to get back to her activities and friends.

"I should call her."

"You should. I know they'd love to have you helping over there. Caroline Cutler can't find her behind with both hands."

Pamela's laugh was knowing and sadly rusty. It made it worth having to deal with Nancy just to get that response.

But Nancy didn't want to let go of a chance to fight. "Rushing off so soon? Busy life of leisure you've got here?"

"Chris has an after-school thing with his tutor." She pointedly ignored her sister. "But I'll pick him up at four thirty from there."

"Thank you, honey."

"If you're gone when I return, have a safe trip home."

"I'm spending the night. Wish I'd thought of cleaning out the apartment over the garage. Must be pretty cozy up there."

But that would have taken work. Effort. Never would have happened as her sister was a total loser, which went hand-in-hand with lazy.

"It sure is. Thanks for asking." Her smile was forced, she knew, but she brushed a kiss over her mother's cheek.

She escaped quickly, almost feeling bad for leaving their mother with Nancy. But not *that* bad. Anyway, she had an appointment at Tate's salon to have Anne cut her hair, and she wasn't going to miss that to hang out and trade insults with her sister.

"Hey, ladies. And you too, Beth," Lily called out as she entered the salon.

Beth hooted a laugh and tossed a curler at her, which she caught handily. "Nancy's in my mother's living room. I need some prettifying to take my mind off that."

Anne waved her to the shampoo station. "Come on then. I'll massage your scalp with the pretty-smelling stuff and cut your hair. I've been telling Tate we should serve wine, I think this is one of those perfect examples why."

She let her muscles relax, breathing out slowly. "I'm dumb to let her get to me."

"Girl, Nancy wouldn't be happy if Jesus hisself came down and handed her a five-dollar bill." Beth sniffed and Lily laughed.

Anne draped her clothing to protect her from the water and excess hair and had Lily lean back. "Close your eyes and tell us about it."

The shop was empty at the moment so Beth and Tate were standing nearby, listening.

The water was the perfect temperature. The scent of the shampoo was sort of tropical and lifted her spirits. "I think I love you, Anne Murphy."

Anne laughed.

She filled them in on that day's business with her sister.

"Why is she that way? I don't get it. You're not, and you had the same parents and the same upbringing." Anne helped her up and to the chair where she towel dried Lily's hair and began to section it off to cut.

"I don't know. She's always been this way. Closest to our

father, so that probably explains most of it. But she's never happy. Given the opportunity to smile or frown, she'll frown. She will always choose to be casually vicious because I think it's the only way she knows how to be."

"You had a good stylist in Macon." Anne met Lily's eyes in the mirror. "Not as good as me, though." She winked. "What are you looking for?"

"What do you suggest?"

"She's got that vintage thing going and it works for her." Tate cocked her head and looked Lily over carefully.

"Are you looking to keep it or do something totally new? I agree with Tate that the vintage thing works for you. I can take it shorter, like a chin-length bob. Keep it longer so you can do pin curls and that sort of thing."

"I want it easy on most days with the ability to do something more when I have the time. It's got a natural wave so it takes me forever to straighten when it's very short."

"Okay then. I've got it." Anne began to work, and Beth perched next to them as Tate went to deal with a client.

"We're on for Saturday night, right? I'm still pouting you didn't come to the cookout last weekend. How was Macon?"

"Yes we're on. I haven't bowled in a million years so that will be my excuse for sucking. Just telling you that in advance. As for Macon? Looks like my condo is going to sell. Big relief there. Oh! I found out two of my prints sold so that'll cover some bills. Spoke with my boss and he's going to send some freelancing work my way again. I told him this move was permanent, and he'll probably have to let me go to get a local. But he's open to my doing contract work and that's a plus."

"Have you given any serious thought about doing portraits for people?" Beth shifted and put a mug of tea into Lily's hands. "Not wine, but chamomile. It'll help some."

"I used to do it on the side for extra money. I may again. Right now, especially until the end of the school year, my focus is Chris. But then I'll have to re-evaluate my long-term job stuff."

She did feel better after the tea. Mainly it was being surrounded by her friends and being able to vent about Nancy. But the new haircut was good too. She felt younger and lighter.

"What do you think?" Anne stood back, holding the mirror up so Lily could see the back. She'd styled it into big, lush waves. "I know you know how to do this one. I've seen you in it. But even when you don't want to do the waves, you can still do a quick style and go."

"I like it."

He could *not* be there.

But he was. Her heart skipped a few beats as she took Nathan in from the tips of his boots up to that face of his. Lordamighty he was a good-looking man.

A good-looking man who seemed to show up everywhere she was in town.

"I'd say, fancy seeing you here. But I get the distinct feeling it's not a coincidence at all." She cut her gaze to Beth, who busied herself tidying up.

"Don't have any idea what you mean." He grinned, and her panties tried to jump from her rear end at the sight. "I was just stopping in after school to say hello to all my sisters. Your being here is a bonus."

She paid and ignored Anne's squawking about the tip being too much. "Thank you, Murphy ladies, for the tea, the sympathy and the hairdo. Yes, Beth, I'll see you Saturday." She tried to rush past but he followed her out.

"Have dinner with me."

"Nathan, we can't have dinner. I'm due home for dinner. I've got to run to the school to pick Chris up, and then we're getting a pizza to bring back home." She should probably order extra since Nancy was around.

"Tomorrow then."

She wanted to say no, punch him in the stones and walk away. But she wouldn't, because the part of her that wanted to say yes was far greater.

"Look, we've said all we need to say."

"No we haven't. And it's not about that anyway. Not entirely. I want to catch up. Talk about Chris. It's just a dinner. The Sands? Five? It'll still be broad daylight. Full of seniors getting the early bird special, but the pie will be fresh. I haven't forgotten how much you like peach pie."

She sighed. He made her weak. Made her wish for things she tried to convince herself not to want.

"It's not a date."

He grinned, triumphant, reminding himself to send a huge bouquet of flowers to his sisters the following day.

"Of course not. Just dinner between old friends." He'd work on the date stuff later. But when he'd fallen for her originally, it had been after he'd gotten to know her as a friend. It had a certain lovely rhythm that he'd get to know her again and hopefully get that second chance.

"I'll see you at five." She walked down the steps and toward her car. "Not. A. Date."

Feeling like an idiot, he looked at himself in the mirror for the dozenth time. He'd actually changed clothes already. Twice. This was approaching utter fail status, and he needed to get his head into the game or he'd blow this chance.

Before, when they'd been together he never would have been this nervous. She'd always felt natural to him. They'd been friends a long time and when it moved to something else, it had been easy.

But now. He checked the mirror. Now he knew just how he approached this thing, how he handled himself with all the right groveling and wooing was integral. No time to rest on being handsome or charming. She'd been there and done that.

Beth breezed in like he didn't have his front door closed for a reason. "Hey." She looked him up and down, ignoring his annoyance. "Nice. Don't wear that jacket. You look like you're going to a funeral in that thing."

"Is your hand broken?"

She gave him the finger. "I don't need to knock on your door because I'm here to give you some advice."

He looked at her warily and she laughed. "Is this like that time you came to the movies and sat behind me and my date and kicked my seat the whole night?"

She grinned again. "Ah, good times. If I recall correctly, Lily was with me that day. Anyway, I'm not here to torment you for your bad choices. Not tonight at least. Look, as annoying as you are and all, you're a good guy and Lily is a great woman and even though you screwed up big time you both deserve a second shot. If you mess it up I'm telling Tate on you."

"Mmm-hmm. So what's this advice then?"

"It's that you never tried to talk to her. After she caught you with your floozie. Her freaking cousin!"

"She wasn't my anything." He glared but she was a Murphy and therefore made of sterner stuff. Her response was a bland, bored look. "Thank you for telling me that," he amended.

"Don't wear that shirt." She headed to the closet and tossed him the one he'd been wearing first. "This one is nice on you. Makes you look handsome in that non-threatening way."

"If I wear it will you stop pestering me?"

"Hell no. But I will for now."

He snorted and took the shirt. "Now go or you might see something you'll have to tell a therapist about."

She sniffed with mock indignance. "Your scrawny chest is nothing to write home about. If you mess this up, I will be so mad at you."

He pulled the shirt on quickly and then hugged her. "I'll try not to be a dumbass."

"Big challenge but you do have that big-city diploma and all." She looked him over. "Nice. Handsome. You have all your teeth. Also a plus. I'm all about these little glass-half-full moments, Nathan."

They walked out to his car, and she gave him a look and another warning before he drove away.

It wasn't his first date, for God's sake. He'd had unlawful carnal knowledge of this woman. More than once.

Heat flashed through him at the memory of what they were like together. Of what she'd been like, all curves and valleys. So pretty naked. The kind of woman who liked to laugh when she had sex.

He really needed to stop thinking of that. He walked in the diner's front door and waved at a few people in that way you do when you don't want to be interrupted. Thank heaven none of his students were in the place.

He grabbed a booth fronting Main and waited, totally not thinking about how he'd been the first to teach her all sorts of things.

When she came in, his heart sped and he sat up, caught in her pull. She looked like a freaking movie star off the set of an old movie. A fitted skirt to just past her knees, a blouse and then a belted coat to match the skirt. Pumps that made her a good four inches higher. That sway as she moved toward him was like magic.

Bam, bam, bam, her hips switched. Her hair was done in those big forties-style waves. Deep-red lipstick. Holy shit.

But her look was apologetic as he stood while she slid into the booth.

"I'm sorry. I meant to go back home to change but things ran late."

"Wow. What is it you're apologizing for? Sugar, you look amazing."

She paused, surprised pleasure washing over her face. "Thank you." She slipped from the jacket and folded it carefully. "A friend of mine, also a photographer, did some shots of me in some of the clothes I make."

"Do you need a menu? Oh, hey there, Mr. Murphy." Their server, clearly a third-generation Sands, was in his first-period AP English-lit class.

"Hello there, Derek." Nathan looked back to Lily. "Do you need a menu?"

Lily turned her smile on the kid. Nathan nearly swallowed his tongue at how pretty she was when she smiled. "Heck no. I'd like the pot roast with greens and scalloped potatoes. Tea and what's the pie situation? Do I need to stake out some lemon meringue?" She was teasing, not inappropriate at all, but Derek there seemed struck dumb.

The boy was simply ensorcelled by all that abundance of feminine beauty. He sputtered and gulped.

Nathan interrupted to give the kid a break. "I see you still consider pie a food group." He grinned at Lily, who blushed. "I'll have the chicken. Sweet potatoes and some corn bread. Tea and a slice of the pecan for me. With ice cream."

Once the boy was out of range, Nathan turned back to Lily, laughing. "That boy might hurt himself you got him so twisted up."

"I was going to go home but then I'd have been late and you might have thought I wasn't coming, and I didn't want to hurt your feelings." She looked less than pleased at the last bit. But he liked it just fine.

"You make clothes?" He steered her back to the conversation they'd been having earlier.

"Oh, yes. I do. I made what I'm wearing. Anyway," she continued as if it wasn't an amazing thing that she'd made the clothing she wore, "two years ago I started making a limited number of outfits and separates every year. I have a consignment place in Macon that I work with. They sell my stuff there and I've got word-of-mouth clients."

She sipped her freshly delivered tea before continuing.

"But Beth suggested I set up a little website. Nothing too fancy, just pictures of the items I had in stock and also some of the other pieces I've made in the past to be special ordered. There are different places online—crafting communities and the like—and I can have my store listed there as well." She shrugged. "So a friend of mine, another photographer I know, owed me a big favor and today he paid up by taking pictures of me for the website. I'll need a way to make a living here. The extra money will be helpful."

"I guess I was wrong." About so many things.

"About what?"

"I was just wondering if you'd be back to Macon again once

the situation with Chris evened out. I figured you would."

"I told you I was back for good."

"You did. I misjudged you." He paused when their food arrived.

"I missed this place." She looked around, avoiding the subject. He let her. For the moment.

"I lived in Atlanta for school and liked it. I've traveled around the country and even went to Italy three years ago, but Petal is home. How's your mom holding up?"

She sighed and forked up some potatoes. "Some days she's close to the woman she was when I was growing up. Those are the days I think she'll pull her head out of her behind and get her life in order. Some days she's stuck in a bottle with a handful of pills. Christ. I don't know what to do with her."

"I take it your dad isn't any help."

"If only I happened to be a twenty-year-old looking to cash in." Her laugh was laced in irony. "He told me to take out a loan to send Chris to military school."

He had his own crazy, selfish, abusive parents, but hers were worse to his mind. There was no reason for a good kid like Chris to have fallen behind the way he had. No reason for it to have gone on for so long before Pamela admitted she needed some help. And for any man to turn his back on his own child so he could keep on getting some young thing in his bed? Nathan wanted to punch the guy right in the face.

"You're making a difference with him. He's much calmer. His work is better. Consistent. He's not so sullen and angry all the time."

"It's that program you recommended, actually."

Nathan had told Lily about an afterschool tutoring and mentoring program. It was therapeutic, the adults were experts in one field or another, and the other kids were often facing troubles at home like Chris, or worse. The older ones, the tutors, were kids who'd overcome those troubles. It was a great option. One that would have been cut had it not been for a fundraising drive Tate's mother-in-law held last fall. Polly Chase had been able to raise enough to keep the program for two days a week—once in the middle school and once in the high school—for the next two academic years.

"Glad to hear it. Tim does some volunteer work, takes on some of the older kids who may be interested in filling journeyman positions with local businesses like his."

She smiled at him. A real smile, like the one she'd given Derek, and it made him miss what they'd had, that easiness between them.

"Really? I'm not surprised. He's hanging out with some kids I think will be better for him in the long run. It's been a month or so, but I'm cautiously hopeful. I've been very grateful for all the support he's received from the school."

"Is your sister not helping at all?"

"Is that a rhetorical question? She's still telling our mother to hold on, that our father will finish up with his little friend and come back. The worst part is, I think my mother believes it. He's so mean to her, it would be the worst thing possible for her to go back. But..." She shook her head and ate for a while. "It's none of my business if she does. But I think it would be bad for Chris to have our father in and out of his life. Parenthood isn't a place you visit when you get bored."

"You're right. He's lucky to have you." And he was.

"He's my family."

"Yes, he is. But a lot of people don't put the same meaning into it that you do."

"Or you."

Really she was irresistible.

"I was wrong not to at least try to explain what happened."

She began to speak, but he held a hand up.

"Please let me say this."

"It's too late."

"Even so. Look, I was stupid. Egotistical. The kiss was nothing to me. It was a moment, not even a moment, and I was pushing her back when you came in. I was dumb and she was dumb and she kissed me and I kissed her back. I told you while we were on a break that I'd not see anyone else and but for that moment, I didn't break my promise. But I *did* break it and then I didn't own it. And then you left and I told myself I didn't need you because it was just a stupid thing and you didn't even want to hear what I had to say. When really it was that I was an ass and felt guilty and resented that.

"And the longer it went unspoken, the harder it got until I just didn't do it, and then you finished school and left Atlanta and I finished school and came back to Petal. I should have gone to you. I should have explained. I should have told you then that I was being a dick and that I was sorry. I should have begged you to take me back. But I didn't and here you sit and I miss you, Lil. I miss you so much that every time I see you it takes all my strength not to touch you like I once did."

She watched him, her emotions clear in her expression. He wanted to make her laugh again. Wanted her to watch him hungrily, the way she once did. Wanted her to trust him.

"I made a lot of mistakes. I was careless with your heart when I should have cherished it. I'm sorry. I'm sorry because I was wrong. I'm sorry because I didn't respect you. I'm sorry because I lost you and not just as my girlfriend, but as a friend."

She ate for a time after he finished his apology. An apology she'd have given anything to hear those years before. Never in her life had she hurt as much as she had when she saw him around after that night and he never said a word to her.

"You made me feel like what we had, like what I felt was a lie. It took me a long time to get over you. But we were broken up already. You were clearly not happy enough and we've both moved on."

Ha.

"I'd like to try again. I'd like to see you, date you. We're older now. I'm different than the jerk I was then, and you're older and wiser too. I think we could take it slow and make it work this time. What do you say? We could start with a real date this Saturday. We could go dancing at the Tonk."

There they sat and she liked him. *Still.* He was funny and charming and sweet even. He'd helped her with Chris, and his apology, though late, was genuine. She knew him enough to understand it in his words.

People made mistakes. She made them too. And she was so tired of avoiding him. But it wasn't wise to let him back into her heart. He had too much power over her, and she hadn't been lying when she told him it took her a long time to get over it. She never wanted to feel that kind of misery again. Ever.

"I accept your apology. But we can't date."

His gorgeous features darkened.

He was as alpha as they came. Used to getting his own way. It was gloriously sexy, but she had enough to manage. He was a man now, not even a young man in graduate school. He'd be even worse. Which would mean he was way hotter in bed, but she wasn't going to think about that. Much. At all. Ever in the next ten minutes.

"You still don't like being told no, I see."

That broke his sour expression. "Why can't we date?"

She was totally going to have to make up for the whopper she was about to tell. "First because I'm over you. Second, and far more importantly, because my brother is in your class. He's got enough to deal with right now. The last thing he needs is to have anyone think he's getting special treatment because you're dating his sister. Or for him to worry you'll retaliate if we broke things off."

He growled a sigh, and her insides got all warm and gooey. She really needed to date nice men who didn't growl.

"Do you really think I'd do that?"

"If I did, I wouldn't have accepted your apology. But this is Petal. Gossip is as common as marshmallows in Jell-O salad. He's had enough, don't you think? My lands, the boy can't even go out for a burger without people knowing his dad left his mom for a girl barely older than him. I can't be part of anything that would harm him even more."

"You said you were over me."

"I am. Don't smirk. What if your face freezes that way?"

He laughed and she did too. It felt so good to laugh with him after so long.

"I want you back, Lil. I'm telling you that up front. Just so you won't be surprised when I get you back."

It wouldn't do to smile at him and encourage this silly behavior, but she did anyway because she'd clearly been dropped on her head as a child.

Pie arrived and she was glad for the interruption. And the pie of course.

"I need to get back home. I'm glad we cleared the air and all."

She tried to pay half but he pushed the cash back her way. "I invited you, I'll pay. I'll walk you to your car too."

Plenty of female attention landed on him as they made their way toward the door. That much hadn't changed. It used to leave her feeling a little smug. That he was hers and they could look all day long but he wanted Lily Travis, not any of those other bimbos. And then she was wrong.

"I can get it from here," she said once they'd arrived outside. The evening air was cool, and without even asking, he helped her into the coat.

"I'm sure you can. Where are you parked?" Bold as you please, as if she'd never spoken.

"Around the corner. On Ash."

"Why you parking back there?" He held his arm out and she took it automatically. Once she'd done it, it would have been silly to let go. "It's dark back there."

"It was daylight when I parked. This is Petal. Main was packed."

"You have a cell phone. Next time, text me and I'll come get you."

It was dark but quiet, and the moon overhead was beginning to rise. "I'll do no such thing. And there won't be any next time, Nathan."

He took her keys and unlocked the door for her. "Just keep telling yourself that if it gets you through the day. But we both know that's a bald-faced lie." He stepped closer and her back hit the car.

She was looking for some stern words when he leaned that last distance between them and brushed his lips across hers.

All her stern internal reminders swept away when he pressed his body against hers and she found her fingers in his shirt, holding him to her. His hands slid up her sides, coming to rest at her back, just above her ass.

Her mouth opened on a sigh, and he swallowed the sound, his tongue slipping between her lips like a thief and then he owned her as if they'd never been apart.

She gave in and ran her fingers through his hair as he slid his tongue along hers. He tasted of tea and pie and man. She was lost in the sweet sensation of that kiss until he sucked on her tongue and her nipples hardened to the point of pain, throbbing in time with her clit.

Up the block, someone shut a door, and it was enough to reclaim her senses and put her hand on his chest to push him back a bit.

He broke the kiss and stared at her lips for long moments, his chest heaving as he struggled to breathe.

"I want more of that mouth," he murmured, bending to kiss the side of her jaw.

"I have to go home. I promised Chris I'd watch a movie with him." Her voice was rusty. She licked her lips and he groaned again, putting some distance between them.

"Go on then. I'll see you soon, Lily. We're going to be friends once more, if I can't have friends and then some."

He'd have to be satisfied with that, she told herself as she drove home, because that's all she had to give.

Chapter Six

Lily heard whispered talking and sat up in bed, listening hard.

Quickly, under cover of darkness she got some shoes on and pulled a robe over her pajamas.

It was Chris, on his phone.

She crept closer, not wanting to intrude, but damn it all, the boy had lied to her so often she wanted to be sure it wasn't something she should worry about. And it was after midnight anyway.

"I can't." He paused. "No. Dude, she will totally hunt me down. No, not my mom. She's so doped up half the time she wouldn't even notice. Lily, my sister. Yes, yes the one who jumped the fence."

Lily cringed at his words about their mother. Pamela had her good days, but she struggled through some bad ones too. It wasn't right that Chris saw it enough to know what was happening.

"Are you fucking kidding me? No way. She'd hunt me down!"

One of her brows rose of its own accord as she listened to Chris arguing and wondered what it was over. Also, the F word? No. She wasn't going to get worked up over a shit or damn here and there, but nuh uh no way.

"I gotta go. I'll see you tomorrow. *No,* I have to go. The school calls Lily and she'll find me."

What he didn't know was that she'd hooked him into her family phone network and could locate him that way. A friend in Macon kept track of her teenage daughter that way. If he cut school again she'd totally not only track him down, but drag him back to school by the scruff of his neck and not feel a damn bit bad.

He stood there under the moon until she made some noise and got his attention. "Why don't you come up?" She pointed to her door, and he was about to argue but didn't. "You want some hot chocolate? I got the kind with mini marshmallows."

He nodded as he sat.

She fiddled around with the stove and got the milk heating before she turned her attention to him again. "Something you want to talk to me about?"

"What? Me? No."

"Like say, why you're outside at twelve thirty on a school night?"

"I needed some air. I didn't leave the yard."

"You're not in trouble." She brought out two mugs and got the cocoa ready for the hot milk. "I just thought you might want to share. I'm not entirely bad, you know. I might be able to help with whatever's got you so wound up you need air so long after your bedtime."

"I'm fine."

She poured the milk and stirred, hoping she wasn't messing the whole thing up.

Once she'd settled in at the table with him, she took a sip and forged ahead. "Mom's sometimes a little influenced by her medication."

He rolled his eyes. "She's stoned. I'm not an idiot. I know what it looks like."

Lily couldn't argue. "And that makes you feel, what?"

"What are you a shrink now?"

"Nope. Just a girl whose mom is hurting like hell because her husband left her. A girl who sees her mother take too many pills just to make it through the day."

He cut his gaze to her as he sipped the hot chocolate. "I suppose you're going to say it's okay for her to do it because she's an adult."

"No. I'm going to say I hate it. I think it sucks. I hate that she checks out, and I feel totally alone and helpless. I feel like I'm messing up with you. I resent it and I resent that Dad seems more interested in his teenage girlfriend than us."

Chris blinked his eyes several times, clearly overcome with emotion. "Will she stop, do you think? Or will she be like this forever?"

"I hope not. It's not getting worse, but not better either."

"She fell yesterday and asked me not to tell you." His bottom lip trembled and she hugged him.

"Would you like it if I talked to her about it? I mean, I'm here for good. I was thinking of buying a house here, but I think for now I'll stay in this place. I'm fixing it up already anyway. That way I can keep an eye out. Maybe...well maybe we can get her help. Have her to talk to someone. I don't know. I'm flying blind too."

"Would you? I don't want to make her upset. He makes her upset enough. I know he was here with the girlfriend." His lip curled and Lily couldn't help but laugh.

"I call her that too. Yes, he was here. But don't worry about it. I handled it. He loves you, Chris. It's just...he's not a fully formed person. He doesn't do this stuff to deliberately hurt anyone."

"He just does. Which hurts more. He doesn't care enough about us to stop it. Well, maybe Nancy."

She barely managed to stop from rolling her eyes at the mention of their sister's name. "No, he hurts her too. She just handles it differently."

"She told me I was a way for Mom to hold on to Dad. That's why there are so many years between you and me."

"Nancy is dumb. You know that, right? I think it was that Mom was new to mothering and has no siblings so she dropped Nancy on her head a lot. It's really the best explanation I can think of. She wants more love than she wants to work for. I don't know why she's that way."

"She's mean to you."

That was a way of putting it. "It's her way and that's why she's alone. Don't be like her, baby. She makes a choice to be that way. It doesn't make it hurt less, she just makes other people hurt along with her. Don't let Dad or Mom or anyone make you feel like that."

He put his head on her shoulder, and she laid her cheek against his hair. "I'm here for you. I know you get mad because I push you so hard, but I'm doing it because I love you and I want you to succeed."

"I know," he mumbled, straightening. "But it still sucks."

"Can't win 'em all, kid. You want to sack out here on my couch?"

"You'd be okay with that?"

"Yeah. But I get up at six, just FYI."

He groaned, but went to grab some blankets and a pillow from her linen closet just the same.

She was going to have to talk with her mother after all. Maybe she'd take a trip over to the counselor's office that week to get some advice. But she was clearly the only adult working on all cylinders and it had to be done.

"Hey there, Mrs. Travis." Beth walked up the sidewalk toward where Lily was working the flowerbeds with her mom and Chris. "Chris, you keep getting taller and pretty soon you're gonna bump your noggin on the doorway."

Chris ducked his head on a blush and a mumbled hello. Beth looked bright and lovely that day.

"You're supposed to be at Tate and Matt's right this very moment." She put her hands on her hips, and Lily thought absently that she should get down to the salon to get a manicure that pretty.

"You are?" Her mother looked up from where she had Chris dividing some plants. "Why are you still here?"

Lily stood, dusting her knees off. She was still here because her mother had gone off on a little *woe is me* story about how she was alone all the time and how Nancy said Lily should be with the family more.

But if her mother wanted to play around, she'd take it. "I did call!"

"Yes, yes. But Tate made fried chicken, Lily. Do I need to repeat that?"

"Oh. Well then. I just need to get cleaned up. Take me ten minutes. Mom, why don't I give you a ride over to church? They're having that plant sale and I bet your help would be really appreciated." They'd asked her a few times, including that morning at church, but she'd been embarrassed. Her friends really did appear to miss her though, and Lily knew that they'd help her get past this mess if Pamela would only let them.

"I think you should, Mom." Chris stood and helped their mother up. Lily smiled at the sight of the kid she sometimes wondered if she'd lost forever. Plus she knew he hated yard work.

"Well, maybe so. It does tend to get busy after lunch."

"Great. Why don't you go get cleaned up and I'll take you over when you're ready."

Pamela smiled and agreed before disappearing into the house.

"Good call," Chris told Lily.

Lily looked her brother over. "You want to come with us to Tate's? They're having a big Sunday barbecue."

"Fried chicken. Oh and Polly Chase is there so you're guaranteed a delicious everything. There are other young people around, and I'm pretty sure one of the men would let you do something dangerous near the coals or something."

"So helpful." She sent an exaggerated smile Beth's way.

"Yeah, that'd be cool if it was all right with you guys. Maybe after I could stop by the Shack?" The Shake Shack had been a Petal institution since it opened in the mid 1990s. Kids from the high school often hung out on weekends and evenings. But it was well lit and the wildest thing they got up to was hollering at each other as the cars drove in.

"You've been a pretty solid kiddo for the last few weeks. I think maybe a few hours at the Shack would be a good reward." And the kids he'd started hanging out with would be there. His little ruffian friends would be at the convenience store on the other side of town. She liked keeping them apart.

He shot off inside, and Beth followed her up to her place so she could get changed.

"Nathan's going to be there. You should wear something

that shows off your boobs."

"He's seen them a few times. Also, I don't know why you keep bringing him up. He's a friend and Chris's teacher."

"Whatever. I'll pretend I don't see how you two look at each other then."

"Fine. I'd do the same for you."

"It's inevitable. You two are made to be together."

"I thought we weren't talking about that anymore. All those chemicals have scrambled your brains."

Beth laughed. "You're full of crap."

"Yeah? Well, you kissed Ricky Crandall. And you let him touch your boob."

Beth turned bright red. "I can't believe you took that out of the vault."

"I had to change the subject. I've got loads more. You want to go?"

"Girl, you were no angel yourself!"

They both laughed. "Yes, but you totally let a guy with a mullet feel you up. I win."

"Feel me up! He just touched the outside. He didn't even touch the nipple. It doesn't even count."

"You just keep telling yourself that." Lily took one last look in the mirror and then headed out.

"It's inevitable." Beth sang it as they headed back down to collect Chris and Pamela.

She knew Nathan would be there. Beth didn't have to tell her that. First, he seemed to be everywhere she was these days. Lily cut her gaze to Beth where she stood talking with Tate.

Those Murphy women were part of it, she knew. Funny how every time she was scheduled to be somewhere with any of them, Nathan just happened to show up.

And second, this was a family event so of course he'd be there. When they'd first gotten together, it had been that connection to his siblings that'd drawn her to him the most.

As if he knew she stared, he looked up from where he'd been engaged in a cutthroat game of cards with his brothers and Matt Chase. His grin sent all sorts of naughty and inappropriate signals pinging through her body.

Boy howdy he was pretty.

"Lily Travis!"

She turned to catch sight of Polly Chase click-clacking over. Even at a backyard barbecue she wore toweringly high heels. She was a lovely, if slightly scary woman Lily had known most of her life.

Polly opened her arms, and Lily went, hugging her right back. "Mrs. Chase! It's wonderful to see you. Mom was just talking about you and the project you and the historical society did for the old library. I wanted to tell you that if you needed the services of a photographer I'd love to help."

"Aren't you sweet! Thank you, honey. I most surely will. I'm glad you're back. I know your momma has had a hard time of it. Your brother's looking better than I've seen him look in a long bit of time. Nathan and Beth both tell me it's all down to you."

"Well that's what you do for family."

"No, that's what *you* do for family. Most people wouldn't have bothered. You know, I consider Tate and her brothers and sisters part of my family too. She sure has been good for my boy. A good woman does that. She makes a man want to be better. Be he a boy trying to make his sister happy, or a man

81

like Nathan, who made some big mistakes. You're a good woman, Lily. Make Nathan a better man."

She blushed, but held back her immediate comment. She hadn't been raised to sass an elder. "Nathan already is a good man. And he's Chris's teacher. And our history is complicated. He doesn't need me to be a better person. He's doing just fine."

"Bullpucky, girl. He doesn't *need* you so he can be a better man. He wants to be a better man *because* of you. See, that's how you know it's real. They're all good at talking a woman right out of her drawers." Polly waved that away and then called out a hello back to her husband Edward. "He's the biggest scamp of them all. Why do you think all my boys fell so hard when the right woman came along?"

"You talking about me, lamb?" Edward Chase shook his head as he smiled toward his wife.

She wanted that. More than she'd ever wanted anything. Wanted that sort of connection with someone that made her light up.

Maybe she should try one of those computer-dating things. She deliberately didn't look at Nathan that time.

"I most assuredly am. But it's all good. I save the bad stuff for when I'm mad at you."

Lily laughed and patted Polly's hand where it laid on her arm. "I've always admired what you and Mr. Chase have built."

"Thank you. It's been work, I tell you. I've had my own share of times when I despaired of the man I loved. Wondered if I made the right choice. Wondered if I could forgive something he did." She raised her shoulders briefly. "Any other man on the planet, I'd have probably run from. That one though? He's the one for me. He lets me natter on and on. Nods his head. Remembers the big days. He's a great father and grandfather. A good, solid man who also happens to have great buns and a face that still turns my head. A woman needs that. Needs that to keep her place, you understand what I'm saying?"

"My place?" She'd never had this sort of conversation with her own mother, Lily realized.

"Oh none of that nonsense about a woman's place. A woman's place is wherever she chooses. No, I mean the place you're meant to be. People like to think on marriage or love as something that weighs you down. Holds you back. Marriage *is* an anchor, but in the best ways it can be said. You're a beautiful, smart woman who cares about her family. Right there makes you better than three-quarters of the people on this old earth. Love takes work. Oh sure, you can love someone without trying. But when things get rough, if you don't love someone right down to your toes, it's way too easy to up and leave when they muck things up. And my goodness, they're men, it's part of who they are."

Anyone else and that statement would have seemed dour and maybe even bitter. But from Polly Chase it made sense.

"He's Chris's *teacher*."

"He looks at you like you're the best thing he's ever seen. I've been knowing that boy some time now. I've seen lots and lots of ladies." She paused a moment and then snorted. "Females, don't know about *ladies*. Anyway, I've seen lots of them sniffing around or on his arm. I've never seen him look at a one as if he knew every single detail of her face when he closed his eyes. That's how he looks at you. Anyway, school year will be over soon. And then what'll your excuse be?"

That was a good question.

She had a great time, as did Chris, she noted. He played with the younger kids a while, but once the men invited him to play cards, he was totally happy. It'd do him good to have some strong, smart men in his life.

"He looks like he's having a good time." Beth approached with a soda and handed it Lily's way.

"He does. Heck, how can he not be? He eats nonstop, and the combo between Tate and Mrs. Chase's cooking is magic. Hell, I ate so much food I'm just content to sort of sprawl here on this chair and digest until he's done and wants to go look at girls and have another meal."

Beth laughed and sat next to Lily. "I'm glad you're back."

"Me too."

"You don't miss your life in Macon?"

"I miss having my own house, yes. Having to live with your mother is not always special and fun. But I have some privacy and I'll look for a place of my own once summer arrives and I can judge Chris's school progress on my own. It's important he knows I'm here for the long haul."

"I can see that. I can run Chris over to the Shack if you want to stay here."

"Oh, so I can make out with Nathan in the middle of the yard there?" Lily pointed.

Beth laughed and swatted her hand down. "So you can talk with him. He's dying to get you all to himself. But do you see how well he's doing by not sniffing around after you while Chris is here?"

When Nathan had first discovered his little sister's best friend was a woman instead of an annoying girl—he'd charmed her. Overwhelmed her with the hottest seduction she was sure she'd ever experience. But this lying-in-wait thing he was doing now was even hotter. She knew he was keeping an eye on her. Tracking her as she moved through the party. He'd sat in whatever group she'd been in multiple times, but he'd not done anything overtly romantic to her in Chris's presence.

But he'd sat extra close a few times. Had brushed past her, trailing his fingertips down the back of her arm. Driven her all sorts of nuts. And he *knew* it.

Chris turned and looked to his watch and found her. Lily stood and went over to where he was. "Hey. You still want me to take you over to the Shack?"

"That'd be cool. Thanks." He unfolded his long lanky self to stand and took a moment to look around. "Thanks, Matt, for having me over today."

Matt Chase smiled. "Of course. Any time, Chris. And remember to talk to your teacher about the internship thing. I'm happy to sponsor you if you decide to check out firefighting as a career."

"Thanks! Mr. Murphy, see you tomorrow I guess."

"Definitely." Nathan's smile warmed up all sorts of places.

"I'm going to go say goodbye to everyone," he told her.

"Good idea. Thank-yous too. I'll get my purse and meet you back out here in a few minutes."

He was gone before she finished speaking, and she said her own goodbyes on the way to the house. Where Nathan waited in the dark quiet of the guest bedroom which just so happened to also be the place her purse was. Lying in wait. Sneaky.

She jumped, startled. "Jeeezalou! You scared the crap out of me."

"I've been watching you all afternoon." He stepped to her and her heart pounded.

"You have? Why?"

And then his mouth was on hers. Again.

This kiss wasn't sweet and slow like the one outside her

85

car. This one was hot and wet. A gnash of teeth and lips. His tongue owned her mouth. His hands on her skin, hauling her closer as he kissed her senseless.

He nipped her lip, and she moaned at the sharp, shock of sensation, the pleasure bordering right on pain. A shiver ran through her as he deepened the kiss, pulling her close, his cock at her belly.

It'd been a long time since she'd wanted someone this much. She wished...well she wished a lot of things, mainly right then she wished they were in a place where she could reach down the front of his pants and grab his cock.

The bed was so close. And yet so totally not going to happen. Nathan had to shove all that desire away and force himself to step back before anything went any further and they were discovered, or it went too far.

He sought words as they both stared at each other in the low light.

"You keep doing that." Her voice was a strained whisper.

"I know. And you keep liking it."

"I know. But you can't do it anymore." She grabbed her bag and moved to the door.

"I can and I will, Lily. I've watched you all day. I watch the way you move, listen to the way you talk. You smell good. You *feel* even better. This is meant to happen. You know it and I know it."

She groaned and moved from the room quickly while he struggled to regain his composure. Want had him fisting his hands to keep from touching her again, to keep from running after her. This had to be step-by-step or he'd mess it up. He could wait. Because they *would* end up in bed. It was going to happen whether she wanted to admit it to herself or not. He just had to be patient.

But she was so gorgeous and soft. Fire in her eyes, kindness to her brother in her words and deeds. Patience was a challenge like never before. It wasn't as if he came by it naturally. God knew his parents had none. They did what they wanted whenever they wanted it. And he wasn't that sort of man and Lily sure as hell wasn't that sort of woman.

And so he'd wait and bide his time. She was worth it and so was he.

When he joined everyone outside some minutes later, she'd left with Chris. He felt her absence. He wouldn't have a month ago. But he did now.

"So, you know what I noticed?" Matt asked as Nathan rejoined them at the card table.

"No. But you're going to tell me, so let's get it over with."

Shane snorted a laugh.

"You were gone at the same time Lily went in to get her stuff."

"I said goodbye to her inside."

"Yeah, I'm sure you did." For some reason Shane thought this was hilarious.

"You want her back, obviously. Oh don't get that look on your face, of course Tate told me about before." Matt laid his hand down and everyone groaned at the cards. "I saw my momma talking to her earlier. Your Lily. I'm going to take a guess that it was a push toward you. She's good at that."

"Your mother is a force of nature." Nathan looked at his hand and then back up to Matt. "She cornered me a few days ago. Asked me what my intentions toward Lily were and that I shouldn't toy with a woman as fine as Lily if I didn't mean to be with her for good."

"Course she did." Matt looked to his brothers, who all shrugged back Nathan's way. "She was instrumental in the wooing plan for all us boys. So you plan to woo Lily then?"

"She's not a woman prone to rash decisions. And her reasons for holding me at bay are good ones. Especially when Chris is in my class. The boy has had enough to deal with and she's right to put him first. Lord knows no one else in that family has." He looked at his hand and tossed two cards down to exchange. "Wooing is a good term. She needs a slow seduction because I messed up before. She doesn't trust me all the way."

"You the same guy you were nearly seven years ago?" Matt asked.

"Neither of us are the same people we were then. She's matured a great deal. Grown into herself. She's a confident woman. I like that. She's got a strong sense of what she needs to do and I respect that. I'm older and hopefully wiser. The truth is, I was an idiot before. We were broken up. I didn't truly appreciate what I had. And then she was gone and my life went on and so did hers. Now she's back here in Petal and we both have so much to offer one another."

"So you were friends before? I mean before you ended up together the first time?"

"She was my little sister's best friend. She had Beth stay over at her house a lot. I saw that as a way to keep Beth safe from my father. So mainly I just thought she was a nice kid and all. Until I saw her later. In college. She'd grown up." He grinned. "Filled out. We started going out after a pool party a friend had planned. When she came out of the water, glistening and wet...she had on a blue bikini. I can still remember it. Polka dots. Christ. Anyway, no more thinking of her as my little sister's friend. We were friends and then we were lovers and then we were nothing and I've missed her over the years."

Matt nodded. "The power of seeing those boobs in a bikini would be an awesome one I bet. So you gonna be her friend then first?"

"That's the plan. But I can't seem to stop kissing her every time I get her alone. I don't kiss my friends. Not like that. So yes, I want to be friends again and then lovers, but the not-kissing part is impossible."

"Here's what we're going to do." Matt laid his cards down again much to everyone's annoyance. "I know the Murphys are in on the whole woo thing. I know my momma is too. I propose the Chases and the Murphys unite and make this happen."

Nathan laughed and leaned in. "All right. Here's my general plan."

Chapter Seven

"I don't see why you can't be around more often. Mom needs the help and you're freeloading." Nancy was seated at the kitchen table when Lily walked through her door.

Who was freeloading? Boy did Nancy pick the wrong day to be self-centered. She'd just returned from the counselor's office where they'd discussed ways for Lily to broach her mother's substance-abuse issues. She was wrung out and emotionally on edge.

And totally and utterly done with this nonsense.

"Why are you in my place?"

"Your place? Seems to me this is Mom's place."

Not so much, but nothing she needed to share with Nancy. "Huh. You spend an awful lot of time thinking about this apartment. You might need some help with that. So again, why are you in my place?" She hung her bag up and noted her sister had rummaged through things. "Also, this isn't a garage sale, don't rifle through my stuff. If you want to borrow something, ask."

"Why are you such a bitch?"

"This isn't going to be your day to act like this with me. Just be warned. Now, back to the question. Why. Are. You. Here?"

Nancy started to reply and then apparently thought better of it. Her mouth flattened and she took a moment before speaking. "I need five hundred dollars."

Oh surprise.

"I just had to give up a full-time job to move back here to help Mom. Even if I had a spare five hundred dollars, you still owe me twenty-five hundred dollars from last summer. You are aware of those things called jobs right? I know you're unfamiliar with the concept, but that's how people earn money so they're not constantly asking people for loans they never pay back anyway."

"Things always come so easy for you. You come here and live off Mom, and you can't lend me five hundred dollars?"

"No. I can't. Even if I had it to spare, which I don't. Now, get out."

"I've been telling Dad you're selfish. He agrees."

"Oh does he? Well who better to make moral pronouncements than a man who dumped his long-time wife for an empty-headed pair of fake breasts on legs."

"He's your father! She didn't understand him. You don't know what it was like."

"Oh for God's sake! Neither do you. If he's so great, why aren't you at his house asking for five hundred bucks?" She looked her sister up and down. "Yeah, thought so. Now get out and don't come back in here unless you're invited. Like it or not, this *is* my place. I've got a rental agreement as it happens." She'd done it to protect her mother, but this was an added bonus.

"You think you're so much better than everyone else because you came back to this shithole of a town to help with Chris. But I see right through you. Your life in Macon not what you wanted? Decide to come home and see if you can't get Nathan again? It's not that hard to convince Nathan to have a little fun."

No. There was a lot she'd believe of Nathan, but messing

around with Nancy wasn't one of those things.

Lily opened the door. "Get out, Nancy. I'm not kidding. I don't have to take any of your crap. I didn't when we were kids and I don't now. I don't have to answer to you about any of this." If Nancy had had a purse, Lily would have been worried her sister helped herself to whatever she took a liking to. But she didn't and Lily would lock her door from now on.

"You think you're better than me. Went off to Atlanta and got yerself a diploma. It don't make you special. Some of us had to make our way a lot earlier. They paid for your fancy school so you could come back here and curl your lip and judge me. You got everything handed to you. And you're too selfish to help out your flesh and blood. I bet you've given those Murphys money. But not me."

Unbelievable! Something just broke and all her anger, all the things she'd bitten back over the years began to bubble up.

But as usual, Nancy didn't listen to anything Lily said and the warning she'd given when she walked in had gone right over her head.

"I think you like it when you get to feel superior over other folks. You're slumming here on purpose. Why else? Mom's useless and Chris is going to be a loser. You pretend to be the good daughter but where is all your love for your own father? You can't stand it that he loves me best. That's why you like the Murphys. They're low-rent trash and you love that, don't you?"

"You are a selfish, hateful bitch. I've never in my life met anyone more petty and vicious than you are." Lily had to shove her hands in her pockets before she fisted one and punched her sister in the nose.

"Fuck you, Lily. I'm your sister and you can't even help me? Who's the selfish one?" Nancy's chin jutted out.

"For *years* I've taken your crap. I've loaned you so much

money it's not even funny. I've let you stay in my house, borrow my car. You've never once even said thank you! I'm done. You hear me, Nancy? I am done taking any shit from you. Leave me alone or we can go to it. But you'll lose because you don't even care. You don't even care what you're arguing with me about. You just want to argue for the sake of it. Because you're lonely and bored."

Her sister's face hardened. "I'm lonely? You have no life at all. Shouldn't *you* be married by now? With a passel of kids that you can lord over everyone? But you can't because no one loves you. You got no man and you got no friends. So you come back here and take care of Chris and take credit."

"What happened to you, Nancy? What happened when we were kids to make you this way? If this is what being Dad's favorite gets you, I'm grateful he loves you best. Or that you think he does. Because deep down you know he loves himself and his pecker. You're a distant choice after other women and his own business. Maybe that's why you like to screw married men."

"I never!"

"Bullshit."

"You can't handle the truth, Lily. If we start talking truth, you'll be sorry."

Lily laughed, even as she wanted to cry at what she knew was inevitable. "Bring it the fuck on! Let's go. You're a stranger to the truth, Nancy. Why don't you build a life? Make some friends whose husbands you won't fuck while their backs are turned? Make a life for yourself that's more than just one breakup to the next. Now get your ass out of my place and don't come back."

"I could make trouble for you with Mom."

"You're certainly the kind of person who would use her

93

family to hurt each other because it amused you. Nicely though, I have legal papers both Mom and Dad signed. I'm Chris's guardian. I make the decisions where he's concerned and I don't need your permission for anything. Dad's too busy with his teenage whore and you're too self-obsessed. Mom's having a hard enough time of this. If you hurt her, I will come after you. I'm not the same girl you used to casually abuse. Don't you fuck with me, or I will end you."

The way her sister's face paled was a balm to her annoyance. Lily didn't usually act like this, but it felt so good she wondered why she'd hesitated.

She really had no idea where she was going, just that it was away from Nancy and Petal for a while. Chris was able to work out a deal with his chemistry teacher to make up labs by spending the weekend at a science fair in Nashville. She'd driven him to the bus that morning and he'd seemed excited. More engaged with school than he had been the entire time she'd been back in Petal.

Lily had offered to volunteer but they had enough parents, and Chris had wanted to do it on his own to prove he could. The teacher had her cell number if things went wrong. She knew a few other people who'd be chaperons and they all promised her to keep an eye on Chris too. So she'd taken a deep breath, wished him good luck, and driven away hoping she'd made the right decision.

And then she'd gone back home to find Nancy there. Ugh.

So Lily had found her mother, said she was taking the day to go run errands and headed out of town.

Which is how she found herself standing in the romance section in a bookstore near the center of town in Atlanta. It had been a long time since she'd had nothing pressing but what book to choose and she planned to take her time. Then maybe she'd have a late lunch and some cocktails. Hell, she might even spring for a night in a hotel if she wanted to have a few more than some. She felt weird drinking at home with her mother in the state she was in, but she'd also dropped Pamela off with her friends for some sort of afternoon thingy, and as Polly Chase was involved, Lily felt safe in leaving. Nancy would be frustrated no one was around to listen to her whine and go. Win win, really.

Nathan had been walking down the street. Peering in windows as he'd gone along. A coffee shop. Clothes. Shoes. Candles and then books. He nearly fell over as he jerked himself to a stop when he caught sight of a gleaming, dark head of hair bowed over a book. Long legs, peep-toed shoes, red nails.

Then he realized it was Lily. Which was ridiculous as she wouldn't be in a bookstore on a Friday afternoon. Hell, *he* shouldn't even be there on a Friday afternoon, but it had been an in-service day and he'd finished up two hours before. His little sister Jill had needed something from Tate so he drove to his favorite hotel in the city, checked in for the weekend and then hand-delivered it to her at her job just ten minutes before.

As if he'd said her name aloud, Lily turned and caught sight of him. Smiling at first, and then blinking and cocking her head.

This was fate.

He turned around and headed inside.

Sure she might try to escape, he moved directly to where he'd seen her, and as he'd thought, bumped into her as she was on her way out. "Now lookie here. What are you doing in Atlanta on a Friday afternoon?"

Her sigh was clearly annoyed, which only amused him for some sick reason. "How the hell did you know I would be here? I didn't tell Beth or any of your other meddling siblings."

He laughed, and she sniffed primly and shook her head.

"Coincidence. I had to bring something to Jill and decided to stay here for the weekend. What are you up to?"

"Book shopping. Chris is on the science-fair trip. I wanted to get out of town for the day. Aren't you supposed to be teaching a bunch of ungrateful teens until three?"

He told her about the in-service and then took a gamble.

"Let me take you to lunch."

She paused and he saw the argument on her face. "Please. We're not in Petal. Chris isn't around. I'm not his teacher right now. It's just Lily and Nathan."

She sighed. "All right. I'm hungry though, I warn you. And I need a drink."

"You can tell me why when we get the drinks ordered." He held his arm out and she took it after a hesitation.

They walked and talked, and man had he missed that rhythm they'd had before. It was there, just ready to pick up, and he wondered if she felt it too.

Her scent hung between them as he held her chair out and they sat. Not bothering to try holding back, he leaned close and breathed her in.

He didn't miss the shiver and catch in her breath. He also didn't hide his grin as he sat and took his menu up.

"Why did you decide to stay in Petal to teach?" she asked as they perused the menu.

"My family was there. My brothers and sisters. I knew they'd all be having kids and settling down, and I wanted to be around. I knew the school needed teachers. I taught math for a few years and then humanities and English lit. It's been good to find my place. The principal is good at her job. She cares about the community and the teachers as well as the kids. There are far worse places I could be. Plus I could afford a house after a few years of saving."

They ordered and he turned to her again. "Now tell me why do you need a drink."

Lily took a few bracing gulps first. "My mother lives in a fog of pills washed down with wine. She fell last week and told Chris not to tell me." She paused to take a breath. "She's a wreck, and I have to constantly watch her and try to keep Chris from noticing. But he did notice, and he's a mess and I worry I'm failing him but I'm just making this all up as I go along."

Well that wasn't the story he'd expected at all. Beth had mentioned Mrs. Travis having some problems, but she hadn't been specific and had told him to ask Lily.

He knew a few things about parents who drank too much, but his experience wasn't hers, though it was hard not to frame it all from his perspective. "If she's falling, it's only going to get worse."

"I know. I'm here because she's with her friends all day and Chris is gone. Polly is with them, and she told me on the sly that they all planned to have her stay the night with one of them. I hate that they all know. But I don't know what else to do. Stay there. Which I do, of course. But Chris asked me to talk to her about it, and so I went to the counselor we've seen a few times to run over some ideas with her on how to broach the subject. I get to do that when I return home."

He ached for her. Knowing that pain. Knowing she wanted to help both her mother and her brother. Knowing firsthand that no one could make Pamela stop it unless she wanted to.

"On top of that, my sister was in my apartment when I got back today. She picked a fight. I should have let it go. It's not like she actually cares about what we're arguing over. She just wants to upset me and make me lose my temper. So she won today."

He had a few opinions about the useless Nancy Travis, but he kept them to himself, knowing Lily needed to talk it through.

"I used to think that when we got older we'd get past this. Maybe I'm not trying hard enough. But she's convinced our father is coming back and convinced our mom should take him back. She said some pretty unforgiveable stuff. I replied in like fashion, I guess. Not my finest moment."

"What'd she say?"

"Nancy?" She paused to take a few sips of her drink. "Man that's going to hit me in a few." She smiled up at the server. "Can we get some bruschetta while we're looking at the menu?" The server assured her he'd get right on it and left to make it happen.

"You're good at that." He grinned, putting his menu aside.

"At what?"

"With servers. You smile at them and they only want to please you."

She blushed and then laughed. "Oh yeah, right."

"First at the Sands and right now. You're a beautiful woman and your smile is gorgeous. You were beautiful then too. But now you're more."

She stopped laughing and took him in, clearly weighing what he'd said. And where this was going.

"I want you. You know that." He shrugged.

"Nancy claims you and she dallied." The look on her face told him she thought it was a lie, and he relaxed a little. "I know she's lying. She just wanted to hurt me."

"Would it have? If it was true. Which it isn't." He wished that hadn't sounded as coy as it had.

Again the long pause. "Yes it would have."

That felt good.

"She did come on to me. Several times."

"While we were together?"

The server brought out the bruschetta, took their orders and retreated.

It was his turn to pause because he'd never told her. He hadn't wanted to hurt her then and he sure as hell didn't now. But he had to and he hated it.

"It doesn't matter. She was pitching but I wasn't catching. She's not you, baby. Never. Ever in a million years would she be. I know you might have trouble believing that after the kiss you walked in on. But that's the truth. I didn't even want that kiss. It was one very brief moment when I thought about the alternatives. A half a breath and it was over. But you came in before it was over and then you left. And I was an idiot and this is what got us here. I don't want any lies between us now. I want to make it work this time around. Your sister doesn't have your best interests at heart. She never has."

Lily breathed in deep, and he tried not to groan when she took a bite and then swiped her tongue over her bottom lip to catch some tomato.

"I don't know. She's...difficult. Ugly. Resentful even though she's at fault for her own messes. My mother lets her get away with it. Hell, maybe it's me. Maybe I *have* been handed everything so I'm spoiled."

She finished her drink and he signaled for another. He wanted to fix this for her.

"No. It's not you."

"Why didn't you tell me? When she came on to you."

"I didn't want to hurt you. It didn't mean anything to me." It wasn't as if he'd even considered the rather crudely *repeated* offers from Nancy anyway. He'd always wondered if she'd done it just to hurt Lily and he didn't want any part of that. And Nancy Travis was a pale shadow of her sister. That's why she was so angry and resentful. Lily was vibrant and lovely. Caring.

"And if Tim came on to me? How would you feel about me not telling you?"

He bared his teeth a moment at the thought. "That's different."

One of her brows rose. "It is? Pray tell, how?"

"Tim and I are close. And he's not a psycho like your sister."

She held back a smile but he saw it in her eyes. "That's a lame excuse."

"It is. But it's the one I've got. Now. On to better things. When do you have to be back home?"

Her gaze locked with his. "This is a bad idea, Nathan. We did this before and it didn't work. Took me a long time to get over."

"It could have worked. We had the connection then and you can't deny we still do. I'm older and a lot wiser I hope anyway. You are too. It didn't work because I was a stupid boy. But I'm a man now and I won't lose you again. We're here. I have a room in this very hotel. I want you naked. I want to be in you. I want to know what you taste like now."

Her breath caught and her pupils swallowed the iris.

"I don't have to be back until tomorrow."

Chapter Eight

It had been foolhardy to come back to the hotel with him. She knew it and had zero plans to halt the inevitable between them. Each step they'd taken, it had felt right. She'd fallen into a rhythm with him as they'd talked. One she hadn't realized she'd missed with such ferocity until she had it again.

And now in his room he watched her every move. Looked at her like he wanted to take a big bite. "You're a thrilling man, Nathan Murphy." She swallowed hard and gave over to what she wanted. No more arguing. She wanted him as much as he appeared to want her. And she saw just how much in his gaze, in the swell of his cock against his zipper.

His grin was feral and a shiver went through her. He nearly prowled as he led her back into the bedroom. Fascinating. This man gave off his masculinity in a warm radiant wave. He took up all the air around her, stealing her breath.

"Am I now?" His voice had lowered, and the memories of what came next flooded straight to her pussy.

She nodded and hoped he didn't see the gulp.

He got close enough to touch but hesitated. Teasing. Just barely away. So close the heat of him slid over her skin. And then he licked up the side of her neck and bit her earlobe. That was good enough to make her lock her knees to keep standing.

And he was only getting started.

He'd been a foreplay sort of man before. He'd tease her all night long before they'd fuck. They'd go out on a date and he'd slowly drive her crazy with lingering touches, soft kisses at first.

Hotter and hotter he'd build her up. Sometimes he'd make her come at least three times before they got down to business.

It had been a fine quality in her first real lover.

But *this* Nathan was a grown-up. He owned his power as a man, as a sexual, attractive male in his prime. His attentions were so intense they were nearly physical. "I s'pose you've learned a few things in the last six years or so." Of course her voice was breathy and sort of stuttery.

He paused and threw his head back on a laugh. Unable to stop, she drew closer, tiptoeing up to kiss the hollow of his throat. His laugh died on a near moan, and his hands slid into her hair, sending her combs somewhere else. "I like it down."

Ha! So did she, but he probably meant her hair.

She watched as his fingers undid the buttons of her blouse. "I have, I like to think, worked on my skills. Purely because you should be the best you can be at things."

It was her turn to laugh.

He tipped her head just so, and she closed her eyes as his mouth, hot and wet, found the spot right behind her jaw. She may have whimpered, but it could have been in her head. Nathan's hands on her, his mouth, made her dizzy.

"I do seem to recall that was a spot you were partial to," he murmured, his lips a whisper against her skin as he spoke.

"Yes. You have a good memory."

He bent his head to her again, kissing along her jaw and up to her lips. She wound her arms around him, arching to get closer and certainly not minding the tingles barely shy of pain as she pulled against his hold.

He nipped her bottom lip and slid his tongue over the sting. "You are so good at this."

"Yeah?" He took another kiss, just a brief, but deep slide of lips and tongues. "It's because you taste so good. I can't get enough. I've wanted this, thought about this pretty much nonstop since you walked into my classroom a little over a month ago."

He said the best stuff.

The next kiss wasn't so brief. He left her breathless and dizzy as he stepped back and she stepped forward, not wanting to lose contact.

He touched her and it sent her back but not in the same way it had before. Now she was different. She wished that meant it didn't affect her as deeply, but the opposite was true. The woman knew what this meant. The woman knew this sort of connection was rare.

Knew the absence of that connection as well.

He kissed her shoulder as he bared it, pushing her blouse from her arms. "So beautiful." He looked down at her breasts, and she was mighty glad she'd worn the cute panty and bra set that day.

"These make me want to sigh happily." A brush of his lips over the curve at the top of the right and then the left breast. Two deft moves and the bra was a thing of the past.

"You're very good at that." She sent him a raised brow and received that grin in return. The grin made her shiver with anticipation.

"You have a pierced nipple." He said this with awe in his voice.

"Yes." She had to lick her lips to get the words out. Especially once he pulled just right on the bar.

"When?"

It had been a silly impulse when she'd been visiting a friend in Nashville. She was glad she'd done it though because it made her feel sexy just knowing it was there. Made her feel good when a man knew how to tug on it right. Which was rarer than she'd thought it would be.

Not so Nathan.

"I've had it four years now." She groaned as he licked over the nipple and sucked it into his mouth, his teeth grazing as he did.

"It's sexy."

She smiled, feeling quite sexy right at the moment with his hands all over her and his mouth against the side of her breast.

"You taste good, Lil. I've missed your salt and sweet skin." He licked over each rib and went to his knees, stealing her breath as he slid his hands up her calves and then pulled her close enough to press his face against her pussy through her skirt. Just enough to make her gasp.

"What are you wearing under this skirt?" He said it as he slid the hem up to look himself. "Ah, matching panties. I like that. Not enough to leave them on though." He hooked his fingers on the waistband and pulled down.

She stepped from them, mesmerized by the way he looked there, on his knees, staring at her pussy like it was the loveliest thing he'd ever seen.

There was no shyness with him. Funny that. But she trusted him to find her beautiful. Felt beautiful and sexy when he looked at her. Even so, it nearly drove her to her knees when he licked his lips while drawing closer. A ragged moan tore from her when he pressed a kiss to the inside of her thigh.

"Do you still like having your pussy licked until you make that sound—God that sound—where you sort of gasp and moan?"

"Is that a rhetorical question?"

Again the grin.

"You're not naked."

"I'm afraid if I take my pants off my cock will be in you before I get a chance to do anything else."

She unzipped her skirt and stepped from it, leaving the heels on. "I want to see you, Nathan."

He surged to his feet, and in one quick movement, his shirt was off and wow, was his upper body pretty. She circled him, getting close enough to lick over a nipple, enjoying the way he shivered. "You weren't the only one who's learned a few new tricks. In the interest of skill building of course."

"I'm not sure if I should clap or frown that another man had this view. Shit! Is that...?" He took her arm and looked at her back where a tattoo swirled up her spine. "You have a tattoo and a piercing too?"

She'd bet money his old skeezebot of a fiancé had neither. Ha.

"I do."

"On the bed. Ass at the edge. I *will* make you come on my lips before I get my cock in you. Leave the heels on, I want to feel them against my ass when I'm fucking you."

Hoo boy.

She moved and then sat, watching him get rid of his pants and underwear.

"I'd remember that in a dark room with a blindfold on," she murmured, taking in the sight of long, tall, hard Nathan Murphy with his burnished skin and acres of muscles.

He landed on the bed and pulled her close. "First I want to kiss you awhile."

As if she'd argue?

She rolled against his body and they both paused to draw

105

in a ragged breath as skin slid against skin. "You feel good, baby."

She wanted to be the only woman he remembered this way. Wanted to the one he compared all other women to for the rest of his life, and the way he kissed her, taking a leisurely and yet very thorough tour of her mouth, made her believe that might be the case. At least in some part.

Her hands slid over all that warm, taut skin. She caressed every part of him she could reach as he plundered her mouth with his teeth and tongue. She denied him nothing and he took until she was dizzy with want. Her pussy was wet, so wet she'd have been embarrassed with anyone else. But with him? She knew he'd make it better. Knew he'd ease that ache.

He rolled so she came to rest on top of him, and the memories that had caused her so much pain before softened so that she could enjoy them again. Know that this was different, and yet just as good. Maybe better.

Large, strong hands cupped her ass, holding her in place as he rolled his hips, bringing his cock to slide against the outside of her pussy until she thought she might come just from that.

But he wasn't done.

Nathan was pretty sure he'd embarrass himself something fierce if he put his cock near any warm, wet part of her right at that moment. It was so much just then, having her with him again after so long. Her gorgeous curves naked to his gaze and his touch.

The way she writhed against him was enough to make him clench his jaw, so he rolled her again and loomed above her body to get a better look. The silver bar through her right nipple was a surprise. A hot one at that. Knowing she had a tattoo and a piercing under those clothes of hers would torment his cock forever now. As if he wasn't already tormented every time he caught sight of her around town.

He kissed over that sweet blade of her collarbone, loving the way her fingers slid into his hair and held him to her. On to the nipples, first the unpierced left and then the right where he played with the bar, learning her, pleasing himself as well. Down over the softness of her belly, the scent of her arousal drawing him exactly where he wanted to be.

Sweet Christ, her taste when he drew her thighs apart and took a lick was so good he groaned nearly as loud as she did. Over and over again as he took her higher and higher. Listened to her cues as she tugged his hair to hit certain spots in certain ways. It wasn't the first time he'd gone down on her, but he wanted it to be the best time for her.

When she came, the sounds she made, the sounds she *still* made rocked him to his foundations as he realized he'd been looking for that sound for years to no avail. Rocked him to realize he'd never let go of her and sure as hell wasn't going to now that he had her back.

He looked up the line of her body to see her face. To watch her sleepy eyes widen when he licked his lips.

"I want you in me."

He was up and searching through his toiletries bag in moments, hoping and praying a condom was somewhere to be found. It took him a bit, but he returned to her, victorious.

He was feeling pretty studly until she got to her hands and knees and sent him a look over her shoulder. "Get to it, cowboy."

"You're going to kill me," he said as he ripped the packet with his teeth and got the condom on in seconds flat.

"Yes? But not until after you're finished."

This Lily was more confident than the younger version. It made him even hotter for her, this absolute sense of ownership of her sexuality. Nothing was sexier in his mind than a woman who knew what she wanted and went for it.

"You seem less than worried about the me-being-dead part." He got on the mattress. "Turn around. I want to watch." He indicated the mirror above the dresser across the room.

She turned and then blushed a little before sending him a smile. "All right. And really, as long as you wait until you're done…"

He slapped her ass playfully and forgot all jokes as he spread her open and started the slow push into her body. Watching the pink flush over her skin and the way her breasts jiggled as she squirmed back to meet his thrust was sweet torture. The tattoo on her back was beautiful, and he bent to kiss her spine, having to pause as he seated himself completely inside the inferno-hot embrace of her pussy.

"More," she whispered, meeting his gaze in the mirror.

Gathering her hair back away from her face, he shifted to grip her hips. "Your wish is my command." And began to fuck her in earnest.

He still fit perfectly, as if she were made for him. Now he could believe that. He could believe that this woman with him, the woman whose scent lived in his blood was meant for him. He'd been too young and prideful before. Nathan the man knew just what it meant to have this sort of connection.

He held the words back, wanting to save them for when she might believe them. Knowing her she'd make up reasons to not believe him if he told her what he felt while buried to his balls in her body.

Instead he fell into a rhythm, ramping up the speed and force of his hips as he drew closer to climax. The sounds she made only stripped him of any real control. In her, around her, on her, he knew it was good. Knew he wanted more. His body responded to hers just like the rest of him did.

He slid a hand around the front of her body, finding her still very wet and ready. He brushed his fingertips over her clit, delighting in her gasp. The way she tightened around him brought a grunt of satisfaction. "So good. Lily, come for me again."

She pressed back all the way, taking him in deep and tightened, coming hard and fast, bringing his climax in response as the pleasure of it all inundated him, drowned him until they both collapsed to the mattress, breathing hard.

"Is there any special story about the tattoo?" he asked as they lounged in bed. Tracing over the curls and swirls and the occasional flower, he liked the way her skin felt, liked the weight of her body next to him.

"Not really. I...knew the tattoo artist and had admired his work. I had a picture of this wrought-iron work I really liked with these curves. It stayed with me, so I took it in for him to look at. Later I added the flowers because I wanted a little bit of color."

"Sexy. And *knew* in the biblical sense?"

She laughed and turned to him, presenting him with a bounty of new things to visually feast on. "I don't know that I'd say that. Yes, I dated him a while. But we never...we didn't have..." She laughed again. "We never fucked. We messed around a little, and this is quite detailed and I'm sure you don't actually care. But anyway. I knew him and admired his talent and he did a great job. No great meaning, I just thought it was pretty."

He frowned. "I do care. I shouldn't. Of course you had a life after we split up and all. But I guess I don't like that another man got to be in your bed."

One of her brows rose. "You were engaged to be married. Really, Nathan, Stephanie Prater?" She rolled her eyes and snorted. "I've seen her in town several times now, of course. She did stop to tell me what an awesome lay you were."

Mortification rose. "Tate tried to warn me she was all wrong for me."

"I suppose all that blonde hair and the breasts blinded you to her true nature. Really, Nathan, she's a vile, vile creature."

He knew.

"I know. I'm sorry she said that." He paused. "What did you say back?"

"I told her I knew because I'd been all up in it for two years before she ever came along and I hoped I'd rendered some good training for the boring lay she must have been." Lily smiled brightly, and he laughed and laughed some more, holding her to him.

"I've missed you."

She took a deep breath and tried to move away but he shook his head. "Oh no you don't. No more pushing me away. I know you want me, Lily. I know you like being with me. You can lie to yourself if you want, but you can't lie to me."

"You mesmerized me once and again with your cock. It's like you're carrying four rolls of quarters down the front of your jeans. How can I resist?"

He shook his head. "Baby, you and your sweet nothings will turn a man's head. Anyway, it's more than my apparently massive cock. *Four?* You like me. You like being Nathan and Lily again."

"Look, Nathan, you're still Chris's teacher. In case it's escaped your notice we live in a small town where even what kinds of birds eat at which feeders in which yard are a topic for gossip. Chris has had enough to deal with after what happened with our father. People are still talking about it. I can't do this and make it even worse for him."

"Thank God he's got you." Nathan wasn't all that impressed with Pamela and her parenting. He understood she'd been devastated when her husband up and left, though it was common knowledge he'd been catting around for years. But that was no excuse to just stop being a mother to a teenager. He was convinced that without Lily's intervention things would have gotten far worse for Chris.

"I keep hoping my mother will get her act together."

"That why you decided to stay?"

She made a face, and he knew he was poking her out of her comfort zone. She didn't like to speak ill of her family, he got it and he respected that. She'd already shared negatives about her mother and sister as well. But it was different when it was him. He wanted her to remember, to trust him like she used to.

"He's had enough people fail him. Whatever the reason for it. I had a good mom growing up. Scattered maybe, but she was there after school. Drove me to this and that. And even then my dad was pretty good. Chris is my family. He needs me and that's that. So this thing"—she waved a hand between them—"isn't possible right now."

He canted his hips, brushing his cock against her. "Oh it is. I've got great recovery where you're concerned. And it *is* happening. It happened twice if I recall correctly. And it will happen again. You know it."

She got up and moved to the windows, the light framing her.

111

"We can keep it quiet until the school year ends. He won't be my student anymore. Be with me, Lily." He hated that it sounded as if he was begging. But he needed her. And now that he'd had her in bed again, he wasn't going to let that go. This was it for him. She was the one.

She turned, keeping her distance, which was a good thing because she looked so sexy and tousled he would have been all over her if she'd been within reach.

"We have to keep it quiet. I mean it. I won't hurt him any more than he's already been hurt."

Now that she'd acquiesced, he relaxed into a satisfied man. "Adds some spice I say. Keeping it quiet." And it wasn't that much longer.

"All right. We can keep doing this part."

"This part?"

"The sex part, silly."

Oh did she think so? Did she think he'd look at her face and believe all she wanted was a hot fuck? Did she think he'd ever, for one minute, be satisfied with what his parents had and then proceeded to destroy over decades?

"I'm not interested in you as a quick, furtive fuck."

Lily heard the anger in his voice and moments later figured out why. She moved to him, sliding back into bed and close to him again. Damn it, she still loved him. Probably never stopped. But it wouldn't do to get attached. No. Still, she didn't mean to hurt him. That she'd make a comparison between his drunk of an abusive father and his skank of a mother, even not meaning to, was untenable. "I'm sorry. I didn't mean it that way. You're not him and I'm sure as hell not her. I meant we can..."

"This is how it is, Lily. You aren't just some random woman I'm dating. I'm up front with you right now that I want something deeper. We *have* something deeper. We always have. So don't insult either one of us by saying something stupid. What we have is more than friends. And that's how I like it. We're together."

She sat up, angry herself. "Really? Like before?"

"I deserve that. And more most likely. But things are different. We're different. You're the only woman I want. Full stop. There's no one else. Nothing else, but you. I wouldn't be able to assert that as totally surely as I can now if I hadn't lost it and known what it was to be without you. But secret for a little while or not, we're together, Lily."

Torn between wanting to believe and wanting to deny it, she said nothing as she watched him, so beautiful and male, spread out in bed like the best-looking item on any menu ever.

"I like it when you look at me that way. Say you're with me, Lily."

She sighed. "You broke my heart, Nathan. It took me years to get over you. *Years.* It wasn't the kiss, it was the way you loved me one minute and tossed me away the next. You made me feel like absolutely nothing." That her voice broke as she said the words should have embarrassed her, but it felt good to say. To let him know the outcome of what he'd done.

Good to remind herself that this little fun time in bed was great, but the devastation he left, that she slogged through as a result of his so-called love, had been a heavy burden for some time. She had enough burdens just then.

"All my life, until you, I'd never felt that. Being with you made me feel beautiful. Smart and strong and perfect." She snorted a laugh. "You loved me and then you made me feel like I didn't even exist."

He looked stricken and for a moment she felt bad. But just a moment.

"I'm sorry." He sat up and leaned over to tuck her hair behind an ear. "I never meant to hurt you. I was careless. Careless and selfish and more like my dad than I want to admit. That I made you feel that way when you were so much to me, I'm ashamed of that."

"I didn't wait to hear your explanation. I couldn't see you there with another person. Doing with her what you did with me. I had to go. I never thought you'd..." She shook her head. "It's gone. Done. Past and neither of us can go back and change it."

"Will you let me earn your trust again?"

That was the question, wasn't it? But she was here in his room, naked to him physically and emotionally already. She'd never uttered those words to anyone after they'd broken things off. Sure she talked about it on the surface, but the rejection, feeling like she was totally nothing to him after she'd felt like everything, the shock of it had sent her reeling. Her confidence had taken a hit. She wouldn't be who she was now if he hadn't been such a careless ass.

She'd rebuilt herself and she'd done it for *her*. Not for a man. Not because someone else thought it was a good thing. She'd found a way to believe in herself and she'd done it on her own. She owed that to him in a twisted way.

"I don't know, Nathan. Maybe we can work on it."

"That's all I'm asking."

She snorted. "No it isn't. You want everything and you want it right now."

He blushed and she found herself charmed again, by this man she'd shared so much of her life with. By this man who'd been her friend before her lover and just might be her friend again.

"I have that problem when it comes to you. But I'll try to

114

rein it in." He slid the pad of his thumb over the swell of her bottom lip and sent shivers through her.

He leaned her back to the bed. "I think we should go again. I found two condoms."

Chapter Nine

"I can't believe you're making me do this."

She narrowed her gaze at Chris and handed him a paintbrush. "I'm the only one who gets to say that. You think I wanted to get up on Sunday morning to watch you paint? Now get to work before I change my mind and go get a switch."

He started to argue but apparently the memories of their grandpa and his peach switches to take care of major infractions when they were growing up was enough to get him past that urge.

"You grafitti'd someone's fence because you and your stupid friends thought it'd be fun. Friends you were forbidden to see, I hasten to add. Well now you can paint it to undo your work." She moved to the nearby lawn chair and sat, taking the tea Shannon Belfort had brought out. "Mrs. Belfort here is willing to forgo calling up Sheriff Chase in exchange for this paint job so you'll say thank you ma'am and get working."

To his credit, Chris did exactly that.

Mrs. Belfort chuckled and passed over a plate of cookies. "Needed a painting anyway. My Frank has been bellyaching about this fence for three years. Thank you, Christopher, for taking care of it. Now mind you, if I catch you and those boys here with a spray-paint can again, I'm gonna let the dogs out. You hear?"

Chris nodded and got back to work. He hadn't said which boys he'd been out with, but she'd caught him red handed. Literally red handed—because he'd used red paint and no gloves—and had marched him up to the Belforts' front door and made him apologize and offer to undo his mess.

A silly way to spend a Sunday afternoon she thought. She'd been up late piecing together a pretty coatdress she planned to list on the website she had put together with some great advice from Nathan's sister Jill, who worked at a marketing firm in Atlanta. So far, Lily had sold several pieces already in stock.

Even worse, she was supposed to be over at Tate's at that moment having barbecue and looking at Nathan's butt. But it had to be done and she planned to make Chris paint the fence at home too. This behavior of his would only get worse if they didn't react to it swiftly and with a heavy hand.

Her mother seemed only mildly disturbed, though she'd been supportive enough as Lily had lit into her brother about this sort of behavior. She'd planned to have the big discussion about her mother's deteriorating behavior that morning when Chris would be off with his youth group. She'd do it the following day when he was back in school. It wasn't as if Pamela actually parented Chris anymore anyway.

It made Lily sad and very tired. But there was nothing else to be done but what she was doing.

"I hear you take pictures."

After she got her cookie chewed and swallowed, she nodded. "Yes, something like that." She was good with a camera after all. Had the gear and the ability.

"My youngest just got engaged. He wants pictures. Or, well you know his little girlfriend wants them for the paper and such. What would you charge for such a thing?"

"After my brother ruined your fence?"

Mrs. Belfort laughed and patted Lily's knee. "Honey, my youngest? The one getting hitched? He's broken windows and gotten liquored up in Charlie Duke's barn a time or two. Not

117

many families in Petal who can claim their children never got up to mischief. Then again, not many of 'em would have brought those kids round to make amends neither. Now that we've got that out of the way, what do you charge?"

By the time Chris had finished his painting Lily had booked a session with John Belfort and his bride-to-be for some engagement pictures and had given her card to Mrs. Belfort who also happened to manage the schedule booking for weddings down at the Petal First Baptist church.

Maybe this moving-to-Petal thing could actually work out.

"She cancelled? Again?" Nathan paced as Beth watched him, amused.

"She's got stuff to do. Chris spray painted the Belfort's back fence last night. She made him paint it and so she has to supervise. It's not like she's getting any help from her momma."

"I barely get to see her as it is."

"Look, Nathan, she's got a lot on her plate. You'd do the same in her place and you know it. She's working on her clothing stuff pretty much single-handedly too. Give her a little room to breathe." Beth's eyes narrowed as she dared him to argue with what he already knew.

Tate sent him a look from where she'd been sitting with Lil Beth feeding her. "You don't like not being at the top of her to-do list."

"Well no! I don't. Is it too much to ask?" Cripes, he was planning on asking the woman to marry him, the least he could expect was some attention.

"Yes it is." Tate shrugged and the baby did the same, laughing. Unable to resist, Nathan plucked her up, and she tugged on his ear before snuggling in for a sloppy kiss. "Yum, oatmeal." He grabbed the cloth and got her face clean and then his.

"She's the only one interested in really helping that boy. She's his family. That's what family does. You of all people should know that."

He wanted to hang his head as he was righteously busted. But he resisted, trying not to pout. "I just want to be with her."

"You sound like a two-year-old." Beth stared him down. The disapproval of his sisters never sat well with him and he knew they were right, but he wanted to see her more and it wasn't happening. It had been a week and a half since the last time he'd been able to actually touch her, damn it.

"She asked you to give her some time. She's being reasonable and you're being petulant. It's very unlike you." Tate handed him a cookie he gobbled down after sharing a little bit with the baby.

Not enough apparently as she grabbed his wrist and started to cry when she saw none left.

"You're starving this baby. Clearly." He shot an amused glance to Tate who handed him a graham cracker. Lil Beth examined it closely and then his face as if to say, *Are you serious?*

"The others had nuts in it. These are better for you." Tate gave the baby a stern look.

Lil Beth was her mother's daughter and she narrowed her gaze for a moment back at Tate. "No." She shook her head and he laughed, kissing her cheeks, which seemed to satisfy her for the moment.

"Give the guy a break. He loves her and she's not with him. Makes a man antsy." Matt spoke from his place at the table with Meg, who was coloring.

"Do you love her?" Beth examined him carefully.

He took a deep breath and sighed. "Yeah. Probably. Definitely. Yes, yes, I love her. Heck, I want to marry her. But she holds me at arm's length. I hate that."

"Get over it. You screwed her over. It takes time to trust again. You can't expect her to just go *poof it's over* and then you two are hunky dory. You have to keep with the woo." Matt looked up again. "And for crissake don't go with this marriage stuff until the summer. She's not going to run away. You've got her back. Give her time."

"Ha. You were up on my sister five minutes after you met her."

Matt snorted and looked to Tate with a smile. "Yeah. She gave me a run for my money. I made mistakes too. I seem to remember one of her brothers threw a drink in my face when he thought I'd hurt her feelings."

Nathan barked a laugh, remembering that time at the Pumphouse. "You made her cry. I can't abide any of my ladies crying." He undid a fist that had been in his hair and kissed it. "Of course I'm waiting until summer to propose. But I have intentions with this woman and I aim to keep them. This is serious business. Marriage business. This is not dating. I'm past that with Lily. I want a life with her."

Tate nodded curtly. "Of course you do. Help her instead of making her feel like she's got to try and make everyone happy. She's trying to deal with her momma, her brother and you. All while trying to make a living. She's got enough to juggle. "

He did hang his head then. "You're right."

Tate laughed and took the baby. "Of course I am."

Which is how he managed to finally get her alone just a few

evenings later when he crashed dinner at Beth's house. Crazy loud with Murphy and Chase women, he brought over a box of stuff Beth had been bugging him about.

"Put it in my closet please."

He started to get annoyed when he noticed Lily wasn't in the room and realized most likely his quarry was also in Beth's closet doing something or other. His sister had totally helped him corner his lovely Lily.

"I have a pretty awesome sister. Thanks."

"Don't get anything gross on my clothes or I'll hunt you down." She said it quietly and then turned around and headed back toward the kitchen.

Ah and there she was. He put the box down and moved to where she'd been hanging her coat up.

"Good, you're wearing a skirt." He closed the door behind himself and looked to the one window at the far side of the closet. Closed. Good.

Startled she turned to him and he caught the blush. "Wh-what?" She backed up.

"I've missed you." One handed, he loosened his belt and unzipped his jeans. "And now I aim to remedy it. In part. You wearing panties under that pretty skirt?"

"Wh-what?"

He grinned and he knew it affected her by the way she widened her eyes. "You got anything else to say but what?"

She swallowed hard and then again when he pulled his cock free. "I want you. Right now. No one is going to notice we're gone, not with all the hubbub out there. And even if they did, each and every person here would go out of their way to protect what you and I have."

She bent and produced a bright red pair of panties that she

stepped out of. He took them from her hand and stuffed them in a pocket. "Compliance. I like that."

In two steps her back was against the wall, and he inched her skirt up until he exposed stockings and a garter belt. "Oh you're so sexy I can't stand it. I think about you. About this all the time."

"You're a boy, that's what you all do." Her voice was breathy, which only made him want her more.

He slid his hands up those pretty thighs and snapped one of the straps holding the stockings up. "I like these." He walked his fingers up her thighs until he found the part of her he wanted most right at that moment. Hot and wet. "You're ready for me."

No response this time, just a nodded head. Which was fine with him. He knew what a nod meant and as long as he had the go-ahead, that was enough.

"No time to taste you. That's a cryin' shame."

She stuttered a breath

She should have remembered how much it got him off when she did that. But all the more for him. He stood and pushed her back against the wall. "I want you here. And I want you now. You on board with that?"

There was no argument on her face. Not at all. She hauled him closer and her lips met his, opening to him right away.

As he kissed that sweet mouth he pulled one of her legs up, and she hooked a calf around his waist, bringing him even closer. He growled and she swallowed the sound, whimpering a little until he brushed the heart of her with the head of his cock. Then she stilled and groaned. Her fingers in his hair tightened. "In. In. In."

He had no arguments with that plan. Not a one. And when

he pressed into her pussy, they both hissed at how good it was. But there was no time to luxuriate in that heated wet, just enough time to fuck her hard and fast and spend the rest of the afternoon with her scent on his skin like a secret.

Once fully seated, he met her gaze and never gave it back as he began to fuck her in earnest.

Hard.

Fast.

Deep.

So good he nearly lost his mind, but he held on, needing all of her he could get just then, knowing it might be all he'd have until they could sneak in some time next. She was wily, ridiculously busy, and he had to compete with all sorts of priorities he knew were important, but hated to share her over anyway.

Her muscled calf held him tight. As if he'd move anywhere else but inside her.

"I love it when you take me this way," she whispered into his ear. "I love the denim of your jeans against my naked thighs."

He snarled a curse and dug in deeper. Admittedly, it rang his bell too, that she was partially naked and he had on all his clothes. They needed to explore that further.

But right then he would die if he didn't keep fucking her. Harder and harder until her eyes went half-lidded and glossy, her lips wet from his kisses. "I want you this way all the time. But for now, let's get you coming."

"Mmm. Good idea."

He watched as she slid a hand between them, jumped with the first tightening of her pussy around his cock when he knew she'd found her clit with her fingertips.

"I know you're ready. Take your pleasure. Come all around me."

Her bottom lip caught between her teeth as her gaze remained locked with his. He wanted to look down, to watch her hand as she made herself come. But he couldn't tear himself away from her eyes. From the total honesty she gave him in those stolen moments.

It wasn't long before she got even hotter and wetter, not long before she gasped and then came all around him. Came so hard he saw stars and had to find his own climax. Which had been hovering just at the outer edges of his consciousness, waiting, waiting until the right moment. And as she moved her hand to grip his waist and hold him close, the moment hit hard as he pressed deep and came.

On shaky legs, Lily headed back into the house after she dropped Chris off at school. Today was the day for yet another conversation with her mother. She'd been put off the last time and Lily didn't plan to let her mother dodge the subject again.

"Mom?"

Pamela wandered into the living room. "Yes? Everything all right?"

"No. Not really. Can you sit and talk with me for a bit?"

Pamela sat. "What is it? Is Chris all right?"

"As all right as he can be I guess. It's about you. And through that, about us all. Mom..." She paused, trying to remember the script she'd loosely crafted. "I'd like to talk to you about how many pills you're taking lately. And all the drinking with it."

Pamela's back shot straight and her eyes narrowed. Despite

the circumstances, that flash of fire was a good thing to see. It was nice to know her mother had some fight left in her.

"That's none of your business."

"It wouldn't be if you weren't stumbling and falling because you're so messed up you can't even walk straight."

"Those are prescription pills! You're treating me like I bought drugs on the corner."

"I'm not treating you like anything. I understand those are pills your doctor gave you to deal with the stress of Dad's leaving. And I know how hard it's been for you. Petal is a small town. Everyone knows your business. But they don't judge *you*, not the way they judge him."

"I don't know why you're talking about this. I don't talk to you about what you do."

"Like what? What do I do that has me falling down and hurting myself and asking my son to lie to my daughter about it?"

Her mother blushed. "Chris is having a hard time but he's getting better."

"He'd be a lot better if he wasn't seeing his mother drunk or stoned all the time."

"This conversation is finished. I don't have to make excuses to my daughter about what I do. They're pills my doctor gave me and a few glasses of wine never hurt anyone."

"A few bottles of wine to wash down your meds *has* hurt people. It's hurting you right now. Yes, they're prescription but I checked, you're not supposed to drink when you take them. And you take more than you should at a time. People abuse their medications all the time. You're self-medicating because it hurts. I get that."

"You've been looking at my pills? I forbid it! I won't be

managed like a child. I had enough of that for years."

The counselor had warned Lily about getting involved in arguments that took the focus off the real problem so she steeled herself and tried to keep to the topic. "You've checked out of your son's life. I'm raising him, not you. He's a great kid. You are totally capable of being a good mother. I know that because that's what you were to me. You drink too much, and you shouldn't be combining the alcohol and pills. You're going to not wake up one of these days and then what? How many people does Chris have to lose?"

"What I do is none of your business. Nancy was telling me you'd get this meddlesome and I guess she was right. If you think you can come in here and treat me like you do Christopher, you're out of your mind. You can just get out now if that's your plan."

Nancy. Of course.

"Well, no I can't get out. There's no way I'd leave Chris here with you unsupervised. No way I'd let him discover you in a pool of vomit."

"I told you the oil I made the hush puppies in was bad. That's why I got sick."

"Your body saved you from overdosing. Christ, Mom, I'm not stupid! We ate the hush puppies too. No one else got sick. You have bottles in your room. You're hiding how much you drink now. You know it's bad or you wouldn't be hiding it. This is out of hand. Stop it while you still can. I checked. Your medical insurance covers all sorts of different things. I think you'd benefit by at least seeing the counselor a few times a week. Just to talk to her about all the stuff you can't talk about with me or anyone else. She won't judge you."

"I don't need a psychiatrist! I'm fine. I can stop when I want to. If that's what it takes to shut you up, I will." She stood, her hands shaking with anger.

Lily doubted her mother could simply stop. Not without a place to put all the reasons why she sought the oblivion of her haze to start with. But the counselor had said this would be a probable outcome and that it might take several tries before Pamela truly heard what she was saying.

"You know you can always talk to me too. I'm not going to judge you."

"You're judging me right now! You always judge."

That hurt.

"I want you to be all right. I don't want Chris to see you this way. I don't want Dad to wreck your life any more than he already has. I'm not judging why you do it. I know why you do it. I'm saying your son sees it and I know the mom I had growing up wouldn't want that."

"You said your piece. We're done. I'm a grown woman and I don't need to clear anything with you before I live my life."

Pamela left the room and Lily just sighed. She'd done it. Had no idea if it would help or hurt, but she'd done it and it was all she could do for the moment. If it got worse, she'd have to move to different plans, plans she really hoped she didn't have to go through with. But she'd protect Chris no matter what.

Chapter Ten

When he called her again, it was as she worked on a coatdress she'd been commissioned to make for a bride she'd also taken engagement pictures of a few weeks back.

Her clothing business was bringing some nice and much needed income into her life after her old job had finally ended. Between the clothes and the photography, she was doing all right.

Which was good as it was one less worry and she had so many it made her feel better to be able to cross something else to panic over off her list.

And it kept her busy enough that she didn't have to think about the conversation with her mother earlier that day.

"I'd like to see you."

She smiled, knowing he couldn't see it. "I can't tonight. I have too much to do."

"A girl's gotta eat. Why don't you let me make dinner for you?" He put all his sexy into that voice of his and it brushed over her skin like a caress.

But she couldn't lose herself in his body. In the way he cared about her. Too many risks to run to him when she was upset.

"I've got too much work to do. Really. You can make me dinner another night."

He sighed heavily. "I want to see you."

"It hasn't been that long, you know."

He laughed. "Well, as I'd like to wake up to you every morning and spend all my time with you, long isn't the issue. I want to see you every day."

She wanted to believe it.

"We can see each other Sunday at dinner."

"Sunday is three days from now."

It was her turn to laugh. "You'll survive. Use your hand. And don't forget to give me all the details. Or maybe let me watch another time."

He made that sound of his, the one he used on her and rendered her to goo. "You're killing me."

"I have to go. I'm putting together this dress and it's all hand-sewing work at this point."

"Don't stay up too late. You need to rest."

Oh he was so much. Damn it. Too much to resist. "Thank you. You too. I'll see you later. Sweet dreams."

She wanted to give all that to him. To unload her fears and anger and let him help her be okay. But she was chicken.

So she just kept working and tried not to think of the way he said her name.

She opened her door to find him on her doorstep nearly five hours later.

"What are you doing here?" She yanked him inside, looking around.

"No one saw me. It's dark and your steps are at the back of the house. I even walked so my car isn't around."

"It's midnight! Why are you here?"

"You're upset." He moved to her after locking the door.

Brushing his thumb over her cheek, he peered closely at her face. "You've been crying."

"I don't want to talk just now. I need to sleep."

He looked around at her sewing stuff. "You do. But it doesn't look like you have been."

She didn't want to talk about any of it. Having to confront her mother had been more than enough emotional upheaval for the day.

His gaze went hooded and a shiver ran through her. A delicious awareness of his presence. "Hi."

He smiled. "Hey, Miz Travis." In two steps he was touching her, his hands roving all over her body. "Too many clothes." He unbelted her robe and pushed it from her body, leaving her in nothing more than boxer shorts and a tank top. "Well now. I like this."

She used to wear his boxer shorts back when they were together. She loved to sleep in them.

"Whose are these?" He slid a fingertip inside the waistband and slid it around her body, leaving gooseflesh in his wake.

"Mine. All you guys wear boxer briefs now so I just went and got my own. Why are you here?"

"Because I needed to touch you. I needed to kiss you and sink inside you. I've missed you."

Flattered, she smiled up at him. "We only saw each other two days ago." Heat flashed through her as she remembered that stolen time in Beth's closet.

"But remember, I didn't get to taste you."

She forgot anything she was going to say and didn't bother to argue when he sat her in a nearby chair and got to his knees between her thighs.

He pulled her boxers down and off and simply stared at the

beauty of her body. Her nipples were hard and visible through the threadbare tank she wore. The outline of that sexy piercing showed, thrilling him, making him even more glad he'd taken the risk and finally just gone to her.

"Open your thighs wider. I can't get to all of you unless you let me."

She closed her eyes for a long moment and then complied. More beauty as the dark, slick, pink cleft was bared to his gaze. "Your pussy is so lovely."

Her blush was pretty. Not an embarrassed one, she didn't show any signs of embarrassment with him when it came to sex. Which he appreciated and knew was an important step to their finally being together in reality. Out in the open. No, he knew her reaction was a flattered one.

"Were you wet before I arrived?" He kissed up the inside of her thigh and then cut his gaze to her face, mouth hovering near her pussy.

She shook her head.

"This is all me?" He didn't stop the smile.

She nodded.

"Cat got your tongue, sweetness?"

"You should use yours. On me. Right now."

He chuckled, the breath washing over her clit. She sighed as he pressed a kiss to her clit, her fingers tangling through his hair.

He continued to kiss, open mouthed, that beautiful pussy that was all his. Didn't matter who came between. She was his now and he'd never let her get away again. He wanted to worship this sweet and salty spot forever and ever.

Her clit was hard against his tongue as he drew the flat of it over and then tickled the underside with the tip. Her gate was hot, wet as he slid a fingertip around it a few times until slipping it in deep, and then added another.

So good. Sweet holy fuck she tasted perfect. Like nothing and no one else, and he couldn't seem to get enough. He wasn't a man who shirked away from going down on his partners, but this was different. Whatever it was between them was different and always had been.

He craved her. Craved her taste, the sounds she made as he licked and suckled. Found himself thinking of eating this pretty pussy at least three dozen times a day.

Her thighs began to tremble as he took her higher, not breaking his rhythm. She tugged him closer. His cock stretched the front of his jeans at that. Wanting to be where his fingers were. He forced patience, wanting to make this all about her. Wanting to show her what she was to him.

His eyes may have watered from her grip in his hair when she came in a hot rush against his mouth. But he wanted more. Continued nuzzling and kissing until she hit another climax and finally pushed him back as her chest heaved.

"Now that we've taken the edge off, I propose we get totally naked and get flat so I can fuck you so hard your tits jiggle just the way I like."

Minutes later, he lay on his back with a beautiful woman straddling his body. "Life is good."

She gave him a smile, but he saw the sadness still in her eyes. He was pretty sure he hadn't caused it or she wouldn't be fucking him just then. He'd get her all buttered up first and he'd talk to her about whatever it was.

She rose and fell on him, her hair sliding forward over her shoulders, hiding her face here and there. Her body was tight around his. Wet from his mouth and her climax. The weight of her made him happy, felt right as her inner thighs slid over his hipbones. He wanted her so much it nearly hurt, but when they were like this, nothing else mattered. When they were like this, she was his and he had no doubts of it.

Her nails scraped down over his chest, pausing at his nipples, playing until he writhed with how good it felt. This was a surprise to him. He'd never thought much about his nipples, being so fond of the female variety and all. Leave it to Lily to know though.

She took her time. Slow and deep, teasing him, bringing him into a rhythm only the two of them knew. Seductive. Soft like her skin, and yet heady, sticky and unbelievably hot. She added a swivel and he might have blacked out for just a second it was so good.

"I know you're down there thinking about when you can take over." One corner of her mouth quirked up.

Yes, he liked being in control.

"You're doing just fine for now. I especially like...mmm, yes that little swivel there."

She undulated on him and he thanked the heavens above she took those dance classes in high school. The woman knew how to work her hips to the greatest effect.

He slid his palms up her sides to her breasts, playing with her nipples through the material of the tank. She arched to get closer and her pussy rippled around him when she did.

That's when he couldn't take any more and rolled, flipping them over so he could be on top and in control.

She laughed, but it wasn't mocking.

A laugh that died on a moan when he picked up the pace and began to fuck her in hard, feral digs. Her nails dug into his biceps as she wrapped her legs around his waist to change his angle and get him even deeper.

There was no sound but the blood rushing in his ears and the soft slap of wet flesh meeting. Her skin slid against his, sweat making the friction sweeter until he couldn't take it another second and blew hard, deep inside, her name a plea on his lips.

He petted down her side as she snuggled into his body.

"Now that I'm sated for a few minutes, why don't you tell me about it?"

She sighed. "What do you mean?"

He turned her to face him. "What made you cry? I can see you're upset. What's wrong?"

"I confronted my mother today about the drinking and pills."

"I take it it didn't go well?"

He was trying very hard not to sound like he was upset or pissed off. The way this issue made him react wasn't about her and it wasn't the time for his feelings on it.

"She was defensive." Lily shrugged.

"Did she see she's got a problem?" He doubted it. Hell his father had landed Tate in the hospital with a concussion more than once. And he was still an abusive drunk. Not that they had much to do with him after he'd been caught blackmailing her some years before.

"Maybe I'm overreacting. She's sure there's no problem and who am I to deny her that little bit of peace?"

"Fuck that, Lily. She's got kids. Her son has been in danger of failing all year. He's making you chase him over fences and attend classes with him because she's more concerned about her pills and oblivion than her damned job as a mother."

She huffed a breath and extricated herself, quickly putting her boxers back on and getting some distance. Distance that only made him crankier.

"She's had her entire life upended. He's taken everything from her and she's not a young woman anymore. She's got to face a life as an older woman. Alone. It's hard enough to date when you're in your twenties and thirties, she's sixty-five. Anyway, they're prescription pills."

"God, don't tell me you're getting caught up in her excuses. Lily, addicts always have excuses. It's what enables them to keep abusing their substances of choice. Her problems won't go away because she ignores them. You know that."

"I don't want to talk about this anymore. I'm so very tired of talking about problems." She put her robe on and left the room.

He followed her out. "Won't go away if you ignore them either. What about Chris?"

She threw her hands up. "I'm doing all I can. I'm not a superhero. I gave up a great job to come here and pick up after other people. I'm here. I left everything behind and I'm so exposed and raw and I just don't want to talk about it. Every time I try to help I fuck it up anyway. She's pissed at me. Nancy is using that to try to make trouble, and around all that, I have to keep Chris away from it." Her voice wobbled a little and his belly ached to hear it.

"I'm not trying to make you feel bad." He was messing this up, damn it. "I got my own shit about this issue. It's getting in the way. It's not about you. Not at all. I'm sorry if I'm making you feel worse."

She sighed and flopped into a chair.

"Did they even thank you?"

"Christ. I need to sleep. This is my family, I have to do whatever I can to help Chris, who has no choice. Thank-yous aren't even on my radar. That's not why I'm here. I'm not Nancy."

"I know you're not. But I'll be damned if I don't say they take advantage of you and don't bother with any manners. I hate seeing it. I hate seeing you in pieces because your mother is more interested in a bottle than you. Because your sister is a selfish bitch and cares more about stirring trouble than helping. It's not fair for you to do it all."

"Life's not fair, Nathan. Someone has to clean up the mess and if it's not me, then it's no one, because everyone else is too wrapped up in their own crap. So it doesn't matter that no one thanks me. Or that my mom would rather be stoned all day than be a parent. Or that my sister is a whore who fucks married men and lives off other people. Or that my father is banging a twenty-year-old. None of that matters because the outcome is the same. It still needs to be taken care of and I'm still the only one who's gonna do it. Whining about it won't change that."

"Why is it so impossible for your mother and sister to say thank you for all you're doing? I know Chris is too young to truly get it, but they're not. It's shitty to treat you like the help. Like your sacrifices don't matter. Where would your momma be if you hadn't come? Huh?"

"It's a waste of time to bemoan it. It is what it is."

"It's not a crime to need to lean on someone. To share your burden with me so I can help you. Even just a little bit. They ask too much of you. I hate that."

"Like it was too much that you guys paid for Jill and Jake to go to school and you had to eat dinner with your parents once a year at least and endure all that abuse to get the financial-aid papers signed?"

"What do you know about that?"

"Oh so *you* get to hold stuff back and it's okay? But I've got to rip myself open? It's too much when my family needs it but not yours?"

"That's not what I meant." Well not all the way. "This is spinning out of control. All I'm trying to do is help, and you're attacking me and attempting to start a fight."

She got up and went to the door. "I told you I didn't want any company, that I had to work. And you came to me. *You* came to *me*. If you don't want to fight, just butt the hell out. I'm doing the best I can and I know I'm still messing up. I don't need to be alerted to this all too painful fact."

"Stop pushing me away. I'm just trying to love you." Seeing her so upset broke his heart. He wanted to gather her up to him and run far away.

"I can't do this right now. Please go." Her voice got thin for a moment, tears so clearly close, but she held her arm in front of her body, between them, to hold him back.

"This isn't over. Just because I'm going right now doesn't mean I'm leaving you. I'm not leaving until you admit that."

She made an annoyed growl and he knew that was good enough for the time being. He didn't want any misunderstandings.

"Yes. Of course. I didn't think that." She sounded so miserable he didn't want to say anything else and make her feel worse.

He did stop, close to her body, cupping her cheek. She leaned into his touch. "I love you, Lily. I want to make you happy. Sometimes that won't be the case. But I'm sure as hell going to try. I'll see you soon. I'll be calling tomorrow. Now really do get some sleep."

Chapter Eleven

She watched her mother disappear into the other room and come back with a full glass of tea. When she thought it, she put it in quotes. Because it wasn't tea at all, it was a splash of tea and a lot of bourbon. And she was on her third glass before eight in the morning.

Divorce papers had shown up the day before. Which, if it had been an isolated thing to see her mother this sauced, would be excusable given the circumstances. Only this had become markedly worse in the last week.

"Hey, Chris, can you please run to my place and grab my bag? I think I left it on my kitchen table. My keys are in it."

He was up and out, with one last look toward their mother.

"Do you think he doesn't know?"

"What are you talking about?"

Lily closed her eyes for a moment. "About the bourbon in your glass not being tea."

"That's a lie!"

She got up and went over there. Her mother tried to move out of the way but Lily leaned in and took a sniff. "I can smell it from over there and I can really smell it here." This was more than she could handle. "How long have you been doing this? Since before Dad left? Secret drinking isn't something that happens overnight."

"You've got to stop reading those pamphlets at the doctor's office. So I'm having a cocktail. It's not like I'm swigging from the bottle in front of Chris."

"You're drinking bourbon at seven in the morning. You're hiding bottles. You're denying and defensive when confronted about it. None of these things are normal for people who don't have drinking problems. He can tell. He's not a four-year-old." Lily hated it, but it was time to move to Plan B.

"Only if you told him! I'm careful."

"Here's what's going to happen. You're going to go to the counselor. Today. I'll drive you or you can get a ride, I don't care which as long as you don't drive. You're going to work out with her just what the hell the problem is and you're going to work to fix it. If you don't I'm taking Chris."

Her mother surged to her feet and then wobbled. Disgust and alarm warred in Lily's belly.

"He's my son. You can't take him."

"I've been documenting all this on the advice of an attorney. I've taken pictures of the bottles in the trash. I've watched you fall and puke. I've watched you fall asleep at the kitchen table. I've watched your son despair that his mother has abandoned him just as surely as his father. I will take him and it will be for the best. Dad won't do a thing, especially when he learns this house belongs to me and not you. Even if he did break the trust, it's still not his. Nancy won't help you if you don't have any money. I'm all you've got, Mom."

Chris hollered from the driveway and she moved to the door. "Don't test me. I've had enough. His last day of school is in three days. Then he's off to that wilderness camp my friend runs for three weeks. You can use that time to get yourself straight. Don't blow it." She paused and then turned before she left. "I love you, Mom. I want you to get better. I want to help you. But you have to take the first steps on your own. If losing Chris isn't enough, I can't help you at all. Please do the right thing. He needs you. *I* need you."

She drove Chris to school; trying not to think about the scene she'd just left.

"She's drunk isn't she?"

Lily sighed. "Not yet. But she will be soon. I'm sorry. I've tried to shield you as best I can. But I don't think lying is going to help you much."

"It all started in the months before Dad left. It was all right at first. Just a few nights a week and then every day and then all day long by the first weeks after he'd left. Then the pills. For a while the drinking stopped when she began the pills. I thought they helped her. I guess it started again when I got into trouble."

She pulled into a spot and turned to him. "This is not your fault. Do you understand me? She's our mom and we love her and I want to help her. But her issues are her own. She's a grown woman and she knows better, which is why she hides it. It might be difficult, I've just told her she has to get help or I'm bringing you to live with me. I'll let her stay in the house, but I can't have you there with her. I can't trust her not to burn the place down at this point. I've taken the spark plugs out of her engine so she can't drive. Not that people are inviting her anywhere these days." Her friends had come around less and less as her problems had estranged her from people more often.

"You'd do that? Take me from her even if you know she'd get worse without me around?"

"She's an adult. You're not. I'm one person and I can't fix everyone. You need me and she's an idiot if she can't see you need her too. But if I have to choose, I choose you." It probably made her a monster, but it was something she was willing to be to keep him safe.

But he didn't get angry at her. He leaned over and hugged her tight. For a brief time he felt so very young and fragile, and she ached for him. "I love you. Thank you for coming. I know I've been a jerk. I'm trying to be better. We can fix her, right?" He sat back and she tried very hard not to cry.

"You're a barely sixteen-year-old boy. You get to be a jerk sometimes. Just sometimes so don't get used to it. And I hope we can help her. I'm doing everything I can. Go to school. I'll see you this afternoon. I'm going to tell you to try not to worry about it, but I know you will. I love you, kiddo."

And he was gone.

She ended up in the Honey Bear, drinking a very large coffee and looking over the shots she'd taken throughout the last week. She'd been so busy she'd barely had time to eat, much less see Nathan. But she knew she was partly avoiding him. She'd begged off the Sunday dinner at the Chase house and had ignored her phone. It was only a matter of time before he came to hunt her down.

And maybe that's what she was waiting for.

"I heard you'd be here." Beth slid into the booth across from Lily, who turned around to see William send her a wave.

"Gonna have to start drinking my coffee elsewhere. You Murphys are far too smart for your own good."

"Nathan was a grumpy asshole all weekend long. You want to tell me why?"

"'Cause he's naturally grumpy with assaholic tendencies?"

Beth laughed. "Well aside from that. Though we both know the man is ridiculously hard to agitate."

"I must be naturally gifted. Anyway, Friday I dropped Chris off at school and went to see Edward Chase. Well not him, but one of his partners. I needed to talk to an attorney about whether or not I could take Chris away from my mother if her drinking got any worse."

Beth heaved a long sigh. "Christ. Really? I'm sorry. So totally sorry. You know I love your mother. She was more a mother to me than my own ever has been."

"But you had Tate, and Tate never would have drank three full glasses of bourbon before eight in the morning and made believe everyone was fooled it was tea."

"No, no you're doing the right thing. I imagine my life would have been a lot different if we'd had someone who was willing to do that for us kids. So what are your options?"

"Today I told her that she needed to see the counselor and figure out a way to get herself healthy again or I'd take Chris. I know my father won't do a thing. Nancy is useless. She doesn't even have a place to live. They said the court would likely ask Chris what he wanted. I didn't tell him that. I don't want to make him choose. I don't want him to have to deal with this at all. I came here to help him and I feel like a total failure. And your brother and I fought because he got in my business and I told him to back off."

"You can't possibly think it's over between the two of you." Beth stole half of Lily's cinnamon roll. "He adores you. I know you love him too, so don't even bother trying to deny it to me."

"You better have taken the half with all the raisins." Lily inspected the remaining bit of the roll and took a bite, satisfied that she was safe from the passel of raisins on the side she'd been avoiding.

"They have cinnamon rolls without raisins here. You do know that, right?"

"I do. But they put more glaze on the raisin ones. Probably to hide the raisins. But I like glaze."

Beth looked at her and raised a brow. "I heard that about you."

She burst out laughing. "What a filthy mind you have. Can't imagine why you're single with a brain as dirty as the one you've got. Cripes. Anyway, I don't think we're broken up. He's respecting my space and I appreciate it."

"It's year end. He's always totally busy with grades, finals and all that. School has a zillion meetings. He's working every day and night too. He's not much of a space giver. I know he messed up before, but other than that, you know I'm telling the truth. He's an up-in-your-business sort of man. And he misses you. He's hurting and worried he pushed you too far."

"I should have known he told you all about it."

"He didn't. He told Tate, who then told me like he knew she would. Boys. So dumb. Anyway, I think you should swing by my house tonight."

"I don't know. I don't want to leave Chris alone with my mom."

"Bring him along. I've got an Xbox and all kinds of violent games that are totally inappropriate for him. I'm ordering pizzas anyway. Come on. You need the break and he likes being around Jake."

Her brother did tend to totally idolize Jacob Murphy, who wasn't quite ten years older than he was. Jake split his time between Kyle Chase's landscaping business and Tim's plumbing business. He was a hard worker and was trying to figure out his future after college. A good influence on Chris.

"If you're sure. And it's not... Well Chris doesn't know about me and Nathan."

"Got it. No one is going to say anything. Nathan has told us all to keep it quiet until the summer. Which is only three days from now, I should remind you. You know, just in case you forgot or something."

"It's a good thing you're not a professional poker player. You lack any sort of subtlety."

"He loves you. He's trying to respect your space and be supportive, and he's a little lost. He's an alpha male trying to be a little more beta, you know? He wants to help you because that's what he does. Help him."

"I'm in so far above my head it's not funny." She scrubbed her hands over her face.

"Stay right here. We need more cinnamon rolls and coffee."

She put her head down on her arms and groaned. Damn Murphys being so wonderful.

"Okay. William sent over the pot here." Beth put the carafe down after refilling both mugs. "And freshly baked cinnamon rolls with extra glaze on the non-raisin ones. He says to ask for extra next time instead of picking the raisins out. He might have been slightly insulted or slightly proud. Hard to say which with that one."

Not much better in the world but a warm-from-the-oven cinnamon roll with a hot cup of coffee.

After she'd eaten another, she sat back. "When he and I broke it off...before, it took me a while to get over it. I sort of fell into a pit of depression. I was *totally* pathetic. God. Anyway. I sat around all day in sweats and watched reality television, all the while just not going to class and risking my enrollment status. Everything was out of control and I saw him everywhere. At the grocery store, at the library or movies. I didn't want to go out. He looked so happy. Man I wanted to slap his face." She focused on Beth again. "Sorry."

"No, don't be. He's my brother and I love him, but I'm your friend too. I'm sorry you didn't feel like you could share this with me before. I was a crappy friend."

Lily shook her head. "No. You were in an awkward position. I didn't bring it to you of my own accord. You never said not to, I just didn't want to put you in the middle and I was embarrassed too. Anyway. I realized one day that my life was not at all what I wanted it to be. And that by allowing it to continue, I was allowing your brother to continue to make me feel like nothing.

"So I made a plan to deal with my credit-card debt, which thankfully wasn't bad. I made myself get up and out of the apartment every day. I studied on a strict schedule, and I stopped eating all the stuff that made me sick. My grades rebounded and I finished near the top of my class. I moved to Macon and landed a great job doing what I loved. My family was near enough that I could see them for all the big stuff but not every day where I'd go crazy, and I'd never have to see or speak to Nathan."

Beth simply listened.

"It's not so much that I wished him ill by that point. Or that I hadn't gotten over him or that he'd given me baggage or whatever. I dated. I had three serious relationships in the time between now and then. The last one I considered marrying. I'm confident of myself and I know what I want. I'm not afraid to go after it either. These are not things I didn't have in great measure when I was with Nathan. But it's because of him that I got stronger."

"And then everything went catawampus."

"Eloquent. So then my parents' marriage breaks up. Which happens. I guess I assumed they'd stick it out. My dad was sort of lazy, and she did everything for him, especially since he

145

retired. I was surprised and I felt bad for my mom and Chris, but it was what happened and I went back to my routine. And then Chris gets in trouble. I come here and in one night I find out this has become such a big problem my mother can't handle it. My sister is a whackjob. I have to come back here and raise not only Chris, but my mother. I have zero control really, and into this maelstrom walks the only man I've ever really loved and he's not the same as before. Not the same in any way that really matters."

"Ah, we get to the in-over-your-head stuff now." Beth nodded sagely.

"He's not someone I can blow off. Not someone I can keep being angry at. He's not someone who'll be contained and under control. He's an aggressive, dominant man and he slides his laid-back, good ol' boy skin on and god damn if that doesn't make him even more irresistible! I don't have any defenses against that. I can't control it, or even predict it. He's like a shark, always moving. He's cagey, your brother."

Beth laughed and patted her hand. "I'm gonna have to tweet that. He is cagey. But he's entirely okay with being laid back and lazy and have people wait on him and do all the work as long as he's all right with the general direction. But once he gets all stirred up, you can't stop him. He will get what he wants. He's relentless about it. He wants you and he's all stirred up. He's changed. You've changed him even more. He's good for you and Lord knows he needs you too. Come to my house for dinner tonight."

Lily heaved a sigh. Still panicked, but not so much she was blind to the truth. "What time should we be there?"

She finished up with Beth and went home. May as well

check in on her mother.

So it wasn't a total surprise to see Nancy's car in the driveway, blocking Lily's spot. She parked on the street and went to her place first, putting her camera and bag away. She gave herself a pep talk in the mirror before heading to the main house.

"'Bout time you showed up."

"Always first thing with you. I hope you give me a gold star in your mental inventory since being disapproving gives you such an extra charge. Did we have an appointment I was unaware of? Something else that would give you any legitimate reason to declare it's about time I showed up as if I'd been making you wait for some ungodly amount of time?"

"You get her all upset and rush off. Threaten to take her child. How dare you!"

She turned, slowly, hands on her hips and took them both in. "How dare I? How dare *she*? How dare she come to the breakfast table with an ice-tea glass filled with bourbon? And refill it three times in the presence of her son who's only just pulling himself out of some pretty deep trouble. How dare she call you in and give you free rein to stir trouble? Did you ask yourself why she'd do that? How about that? Huh? How about she stop hiding behind all this stuff? She brought you here to get in between her and me. You have to know that. She'd rather sit by and watch us fight—yet again—than own her business."

Nancy began to speak but Lily'd had enough. "I told you last time that if you wanted to go we would, but that'd I'd end you. Think very carefully about what you say next. If you're not here to help get her in rehab or at the very least some therapy, then get out. You can't help her with your normal selfish shit. She needs you to be a good person for once in your life. I know you have a heart in there somewhere and I could use your help right now.

"She's in big trouble. Chris saw her fall a month ago. She stumbles around the house, slurring her words, falling asleep anywhere she lands. He sees it every day, no matter how hard I try to clean up after her. He's scared to death she'll try to drive. He asked me if she was drunk this morning on the way to school. He's had enough. She's had enough and I'm not going to let you make this all worse. I don't have the energy to parent you too, so you're going to have to stand on your own two feet for a change 'cause Dad's not interested, no matter how good or pretty you are. It's about him, not you."

Nancy closed her mouth with a snap.

She turned to her mother, who looked slightly abashed. "Now, Mom, aside from calling Nancy and attempting to set us against each other to keep the heat off you, what are you going to do about what we discussed this morning? I can drive you over to the therapist's office now. They have group sessions and individual ones. She said you might need both or one or the other. She's referred you to someone else in her office who deals with substance-abuse issues more regularly."

Her mother looked back and forth between them. "Nancy, do you hear this?"

Her sister exhaled and slumped down onto the couch. "She really drank bourbon at breakfast in front of Chris?"

A little afraid to be heartened by her sister's response just yet, Lily walked over to the pantry and pulled out a drawer, removing it entirely. "Here's one of her favorite spots." She produced the bottle she knew was hidden there. "I found this one when I slammed the drawer too hard and it made a funny sound. There are others back here. I pour them out. Sometimes I water them down. She can't say anything to me of course, because if she admits she's hiding liquor bottles she has to admit she's got a problem. I found a bottle in the linen closet yesterday. A few in her car. She's in trouble, Nancy. I could really use your help."

Nancy pulled out a cigarette and instead of chiding her, Lily let her have it. God knew she felt like a smoke just then and she'd never been a smoker. Her sister sat and drew the smoke into her lungs, not saying anything. She looked around the room, her gaze flitting from space to space.

Lily continued to think on her options.

"Lily, why don't you clean up in here more? Or make Chris." The tone wasn't as hostile, but the wary way she sized everything up had gone. She was paying attention now.

Lily saw the room from her sister's perspective. Pamela Travis's curtains had always been open during the day. But it'd been a while since she'd started telling Lily the light was too much and bothered her eyes.

Dim and cluttered.

"I come in every day after I take Chris to school. I make sure the kitchen is clean and do laundry. Even put it away. But she won't let me vacuum or dust or touch any of the paperwork and magazines on the coffee table. Insists she do it herself."

Lily didn't need to say how ineffective that effort had been.

"Mom, the woman who raised us was proud of her home. She was proud of herself and her appearance."

Nancy's gaze honed in on their mother as Lily pointed that out. All Lily could do was hope Nancy saw what she did.

"You used to get your hair done once a week. You wore pretty clothes. You had lunch with your friends and ran the cakewalk every carnival. You rarely leave the house now. You sit here in the dark all day and with the television on. Staring and drinking. Watching you do this to yourself is breaking my

149

heart."

Pamela, shaking, pointed a finger at Lily. "I don't need any help! I'm just fine. Nancy, you said you'd back me. She's trying to take Christopher. Turn him against me. Those aren't my bottles. She put them there. She wants to control me."

It hit hard. She knew her mother was desperate and in pain and didn't mean what she was saying. But she said it nonetheless. Lily turned herself away from her mother to face Nancy. "Help me. You have to see it. She needs help."

Nancy shook her head and blew out a long puff of smoke. Looking around Lily to their mother, she said, "She's uppity and thinks she's better'n everyone else. But she wouldn't do that. She's right. You're in trouble. You can't do this to Chris."

Chapter Twelve

He'd paced all morning. He'd hit his limit of patience. There would be no more distance. He'd do whatever he needed to do to prove to her they were meant to be together. She was meant to be with him, surely she felt that too. He refused to even entertain that she didn't love him. They'd shared that intensity of connection again.

He'd kept an eye on Chris there at school as best he could. He hadn't slipped back into his previous lazy patterns, but Nathan knew she worried he would.

The boy had brought himself up to a C minus. He'd done a huge amount of work in the time since his sister had come back home. He'd had the lowest grade in the class and now he'd pass. All due to Lily. What an amazing woman she was. She'd dug in and made a difference when most people would have given up.

Things would still be rough. Beth had called him and told him a very sparse account of what they'd spoken about in the Honey Bear and of the situation with Pamela. She'd added that she believed very much that Lily loved him and wanted to be with him. She'd agreed to come to Beth's house that night for dinner knowing he'd be there.

He loved her, this amazing woman. He smiled as he looked up at the clock and made a decision.

School was nearly over and there'd be no reason not to stand under her window holding his boom box if he had to.

Lily pulled into the driveway and worked up the energy to heave herself free and into the direction of her apartment. Her mother had decided to check herself into the hospital for exhaustion and detox. It had been unbelievably painful as she'd hugged Lily, thanking her for the push. She'd looked small and fragile, and Lily had felt like a traitor.

Nancy had drifted off with an incredibly awkward hug after their mother had gone from sight down the hallway. Her help had been unexpected, but in the end, invaluable. And not just to their mother. Funny how sometimes fate could turn your opinion of someone on its ear.

Thankfully Beth picked Chris up from school and took him back to her place until Lily got free. The last thing she wanted to do was have a big dinner with these people who'd most assuredly become her family in the time since she'd been back in Petal. But she supposed it was what she needed, and that's what kept her moving.

She raced home first to take a shower. She desperately needed to wash the day from her skin before she went to see her brother.

Nathan waited on her top step with a pie box from the Sands. She paused midway to look at him. *He'd come to her.* The intensity of her relief brought tears to her eyes. She hadn't allowed herself to really admit how much she needed him to come for her.

"What kind of pie is that?"

"Lemon meringue. I've got a coconut cream too." He pointed to a bag near the door.

Oh someone was getting lucky very soon. "You were supposed to give me some space."

He grinned. "I have a problem with authority. I've known

this since the second grade."

"You did bring pie. That goes a long way in my book. I suppose I can let you in for a slice or two."

She moved past him, breathing him in as she did. She motioned him into the house once she got the door unlocked.

He came in and put the stuff on the kitchen counter near the fridge. "Lock the door."

She wanted to giggle and clap her hands with glee but managed to grin as she hurried to do it.

"Beth said to tell you she and Jake are taking Chris to a movie and pizza. We'll meet them for pizza after the flick. Chris told me he knew I was sweet on you and he thought it was okay as long as I was nice to you. And stuff. Eloquent and heartfelt."

She leaned in to him, burying her face in his neck. His arms wrapped around her and held on tight.

"I've missed you. I'm glad you came for me."

"I would have come earlier when my free period was up but I got sucked into yet another meeting. I'm sorry about your mom. But I'm glad she's getting help."

"I need to shower this day off. Come with me? I'll tell you."

He took her hand and they headed to the bathroom. "I missed you too. It's been hard not to barge in here, to be satisfied with a phone call or texts."

"I was beginning to get annoyed that you hadn't disregarded everything I said and showed up looking just like you do now."

She took her blouse off and tossed it in the laundry.

"I'm going to make every effort not to think about fucking you in every way possible while you tell me. It's going to be a herculean effort, just so you know and can compensate me accordingly afterward."

She tiptoed up for a kiss. "You're good to me." She turned the water on and then got naked.

"I'm coming in. Even if I can't violate you just yet, I want to touch you."

"Damn you're good with that mouth." She stepped under the spray and watched as he undressed to join her.

She closed her eyes and got her hair wet. "Just getting her into the car was interesting. She's strong for a little woman. And then she cried the whole way to the therapist's office about how the neighbors probably saw it and now everyone would think badly of her. She puked in the parking lot once we arrived. Better than in the car I guess.

"Bless the therapist and her colleague, who took us in right away. It went back and forth for a few minutes, but my mom just suddenly said she felt like she was going to lose it. She said she was too tired to think. She's about to break. We could all see it. Even Nancy."

Nathan moved behind her and took the bottle of shampoo from her. "Close your eyes and let me take care of you."

Tenderness sliced through her as she closed her eyes and tipped her head back. Strong fingers massaged her scalp. "She denied and denied and denied. I was so sure she'd leave. And *wham* out of the blue she just tells us she's having a breakdown. It was...difficult. She's not from a generation so understanding about getting mental-health help. She's ashamed of that more than the drinking I think."

He rinsed her hair and then massaged through conditioner. His hands on her felt good. Their chemistry heated up, the tension between them building.

"How long will she be in the hospital?"

"Two weeks for now. They'll monitor her situation and adjust at that point if necessary. I don't know. I hope she'll get the help she needs."

"She's taking a big step. That whole business with your dad took its toll."

"I know. And like I said, once she'd admitted it, she started feeling all the stuff she'd been walling off."

He soaped up his hands and started at her shoulders, slowly moving to her elbow, down her forearm and to her wrist and each finger. All the tension melted away as he did. As he ministered to her. She felt cosseted and adored.

Lily had been walling this off too, she supposed. The fear had kept her from truly accepting what they had and what he could be to her. Stupid to have kept herself away from the beauty of this.

"So naturally she realized all the stuff she'd been doing in front of Chris and the stuff she'd said to me. The guilt is going to be hard for her."

He rinsed her, pausing here and there to kiss a shoulder, an arm or fingertip.

She opened her eyes to find him there, looking at her with such soft love it made her smile.

"Hi."

"Hey."

"Your turn." She switched places kissing over his chest.

He loved the way it felt when she washed his hair. Loved the slick slide of her nipples against his back as she massaged in the shampoo. Loved how it felt to be taken care of. "Sounds like a supremely crappy day. You can have more than one slice of pie."

She laughed. "I have to tell Chris. I gave him a brief rundown over the phone when he got out of school today."

"He seemed very relieved to see a movie and hang with

Jake. Our family cares about him, you know. Like we care about you."

"I know," she murmured as she rinsed his hair. "It gets me through the rough times. I realized earlier that in the relatively short time that I've been back home, I've grown used to this awesome group of people."

"Only two more days, Lily."

She ran soapy hands all over his body and he arched forward when she slipped one down his back, over his ass and balls. And then she fisted his cock with the other hand. A nonsensical sound broke through his lips.

"I know." She began to jerk his cock with one soapy hand and caress his balls with the other.

"You're pretty good at that. Like blue-ribbon, gold-medal good."

"I've got moves you've never seen, boy."

He laughed but didn't stop thrusting. "I can't wait to see more. I aim to claim you all public-like. In two days. Ten minutes after school is out if I can make it here this fast."

"Claim like how?" She tightened her hold just a little, but plenty enough to send him to thisclose from climax.

"Like I'm done with this secret-relationship bullshit. You and I are going to go out for dinner and then to the Tonk. And I will put my hand in your back pocket and smooch up on you and you can finally show the world how much you love it."

She giggled and then he didn't want to come in her shower. He turned, taking her hand. "I want you. Not your hand, your pussy." He picked her up and placed her on the bathmat and followed her.

"I hope you know just how much that move would have gotten any other man a kick to the goolies."

"Good to know my goolies are safe." He took the towel she'd been holding and began to dry her with it. "So you're on board with the open declaration of how-awesome-Lily-Travis-thinks-Nathan-Murphy-is plan?"

She laughed and turned into his arms.

"I can manage it. Probably."

He bent his knees and bumped her with a shoulder and picked her up, his arm banded over her ass.

"You have such a nice behind, Nathan. Have I told you that lately?"

He carried her into the bedroom and tossed her on the bed.

"You can't get mad when I tell you to back off."

She said it very primly and he kept a straight face for a few seconds. "We both know I'm pushy when I need to be. So if you share with me and keep me updated on what's going on and you let me help you, we'll be golden. If you make me push you, I'm going to extract a price."

He leered and she shivered.

"I think I just had a really dirty pirate fantasy."

"What?"

"You looked at me like a very wicked pirate."

"Ah. Well then, girlie. I've come to plunder and ravage." He waggled his brows and she pulled him down to the mattress.

"Thank God. Toys aren't nearly as good as you at plundering."

"Damn it, woman!" He paused to lick over her nipples. "What did we say about not killing me with your dirty mind?"

She fluttered her lashes and reached down for his cock. "I can't remember. Maybe you can help."

He dove on her, kissing over her nipples and down her belly

157

until he reached her pussy. "I love this. So soft and sweet." He fluttered his tongue over her clit and she whimpered.

Settling in, he held her ass in his hands so that he could serve himself, angling her perfectly to meet his mouth. Her fingers tightened in the blankets and she moaned. His cock was so hard he worried he'd come like a fourteen-year-old.

He devoured her, tasting every dip and fold of her pussy. She moved restlessly, her head going side to side as she began to rock her hips, brushing her clit over his lips and tongue exactly how she wanted.

He held her tight against him, delighting in the way she squealed when his fingers dug into the muscle of her ass. So slick and so close, he listened to her breath, knowing she was very, very close.

And then she came so hard she sobbed.

He rolled her over, loving to look at the long, gorgeous line of her spine. The swirls of the tattoo, the flare of her hips. The tattoo was inherently feminine and it suited her curves perfectly. She angled her hips just how he liked it, and when he slipped in, he reminded himself to have a condom talk with her. He wanted to be in her totally naked.

She clutched at the headboard, pushing back at him to meet his thrusts.

"I love seeing you this way. Flushed from sex. Stretched out, eyes glossy, lips wet. The side of your breast makes my mouth water with that little bit of your nipple, enough to see the bar. You're so fucking sexy I get rock hard simply at the thought of you. It's a problem so I have to think about my third-grade teacher to erase any sign of arousal. Works every time."

She snorted.

He fucked into her body slow and easy. He drew it out long and sensual until she writhed at every touch and he would explode if he didn't come. When he did, his face pressed into the sweet hollow where shoulder met neck, he knew he was with the woman he was meant to spend his life with.

"I guess we should have showered afterward." She turned to face him as he came back into the room.

"We're due to meet them for pizza in an hour. I can think of a few ways to take up the time between now and then."

He got back into bed.

"Sounds good."

Chapter Thirteen

She knew he was coming for her. So she took care of errands as she waited. His ten minutes would be closer to a few hours, he'd called to say. She understood.

While her brother was away at camp and her mother was still in the hospital, she let herself enjoy the silence. She'd taken Christopher to the bus for his camp, checked in to be sure Pamela didn't need anything and had even called Nancy to check in on her.

And so now she waited, dressed in her favorite jeans and his favorite red shirt with the heart-shaped snap buttons. The red boots she wore were a barter for one of her tailored dresses. And in a lovely turn, the husband of the customer she'd bartered with had seen Lily's portfolio via his wife and had hired her to photograph his handmade boots for a catalog. Business was looking up.

Things in general were looking up.

"Hey there, Lily Travis." Click-clack-click-clack, Polly Chase approached where Lily had just loaded groceries into her car. She accepted the hug gratefully.

"Mrs. Chase, I wanted to thank you for the basket of books you sent my mother. She said it had all her favorites in it. I know she really appreciated seeing you too. I think she's missing her friends." In fact, Lily truly felt her mother's friends would be the key to her long-term emotional and physical recovery.

"I imagine she might be feeling a little embarrassed. But

frankly I think she's doing the right thing. What woman wouldn't need a little time away when a heapload of manure falls on her life. She already looks better. I'm glad to see it. And little Christopher! Girl, you did a great job with that one."

"I lucked out. He's a good kid. He'll be okay I think. This camp he's going to will teach him survival skills and all sorts of fun stuff. He's talked about nothing but for weeks."

"He's all right then? About your mother?"

She nodded. "He amazes me. He's been supportive and helpful. Looks like he made it to his junior year. So I'll take it day by day." Lily laughed.

"You surely do know how it has to be done. One day at a time because they'll drive you nuts if you don't. I wasn't sure we'd survive all the fighting between Shane and Kyle, but we did and now they're upstanding members of our community. Who'd have thought. All those grandbabies and gorgeous wives. And then of course we gained all the Murphy kids as our own too. Love those children."

"You're smooth."

Polly laughed. "I'm old, honey, which means I get to be rude and everyone makes excuses for me. It's the best. Anyway. I think you and Nathan were made for each other. I know he's been keeping all this secret for you until school is out, but it's out now and I just saw him down the Sands grabbing pie. He told everyone it was for you. Not a time waster, that boy."

Lily hurried. "I'm supposed to meet him at my house shortly. I'll see you on Sunday when I photograph the items for the auction catalog."

Polly hugged her. "Of course. And then for dinner." She kissed Lily's cheek and click-clacked off, waving and calling out orders as she went. "Don't be late or Shane will be grumpy. That boy loves to eat."

Nathan stalked right up to her door and knocked.

She opened with a smile he quickly tasted until he made them both a little wobbly. "Good evening, Miss Travis. Our reservation is in fifteen minutes." He looked her over and was sorry for it. She wore a pair of jeans that showed off miles of legs and her curves all at once. The shirt was exactly what he liked about her wardrobe, a mix of sweet Americana and red-hot siren. Her hair was in two pigtails. Red, shiny lips and big brown eyes. She was one hundred percent dynamite.

"So soon?" She slid a palm up his chest. "I was hoping, you know, for something naked and sweaty first."

He groaned and took her hand, kissing the palm. "Stop that. Minx. We have plans and if I pause to disrobe you, we aren't leaving for the weekend. You're coming to my place tonight so I can debauch you properly at least three times."

"Like I'm gonna argue. Though I will say I'd be just fine going to your place to get started on said evening's plans."

He took her hand and twirled her. "Nope. We got some dancing to do. And a little bit of public marking of territory. Come on. I want everyone to see you and know how lucky I am." He guided her toward the car.

"You're not going to pee on me are you?"

He laughed. "God you're twisted."

"I should hope so. I have to keep my game sharp or the floozies will be after you."

He helped her in and then came to join her, leaning across the seat to get close enough to kiss her. "You're the only floozie I want."

True to his word, he took her to dinner, doting on her,

laughing, kissing her fingertips and letting everyone know they were an item.

Out on the dance floor at the Tonk he pulled her close, swaying. She put her head over his heart, reassured by the beat there. "Doesn't matter who knows. You understand that, right?"

"I do, but for my own reasons. What are yours?"

She looked up into his face. "I love you either way. Doesn't matter who knows it as long as you do."

He grinned and swooped in for a sound kiss. "You do?"

She nodded.

And that's when he dropped to one knee and held up a ring box. "Then make me the happiest man on earth and marry me."

She froze. Her eyes widening. "Nuh-uh! Really? Jeez, Nathan! We've hardly been dating."

A crowd had circled them and a few chuckles sounded.

"Really. And hardly been dating? I've loved you for going on a decade. That's not rushing. I know you, Lily Travis."

That got some awwws.

"I want babies. With you. I want a life. With you. I want you at my side forever. Let me be your man. Tell me you trust me with your heart and our babies."

"I guess so. I mean, I get to have the sex and you living under the same roof so you'll carry heavy stuff and fix gutters and things like that. It's really a good deal."

"I think I'm flattered." He slid the engagement ring on, and the entire room hooted and hollered, celebrating along with them.

Beth stood up at the edge of the dance floor. "To second chances and friends!"

Nathan dipped her. "To love."

"I'll drink to that." He pulled her to stand and led her back toward the table where her friends and family sat.

Her future looked bumpy at times. But oh so very bright.

From friends to lovers, to friends to lovers again. Second chances and reunions all in one. Nathan Murphy was her past and her future, and she couldn't wait to see what tomorrow would bring.

Alone Time

A Visit to Petal, Part One

Lauren Dane

Dedication

This is for the Petal fans, past, present and future. You believe in these characters, you've loved this town and her people, and you've made it possible for me to keep on coming back.

Chapter One

Shane pulled into his parents' driveway and in the backseat, applause broke out.

"Way to make your daddy feel appreciated."

Edward, better known in the family as Ward, laughed like that was the most hilarious thing he'd ever heard. Then again, the boy was three so it wasn't as if he had a lot of experience.

Shane got out and began to unbuckle his son from the car seat. But as he knew would happen, his mother burst from the front door, waving and calling to her grandson.

"There's Grammy's boy. Come on over here and give me a great big hug, baby." She knelt and held her arms out, and Ward scrambled from his father's hold to run into that hug.

"I know I'm not as good as Grammy, but give Poppa some sugar anyway." Edward Chase had ambled over and Ward threw his arms around his grandfather's knees.

Polly stood, smiling at her oldest son. "Come on in. You didn't need to bring over a darned thing. You know all my grandbabies have plenty here." Polly held Ward's hand as they took the big front steps slowly.

This was true of course. His parents had taken two of the bedrooms and made them into rooms for their increasing number of grandchildren. He and Cassie had one, Tate and Matt had two, Liv and Marc also had two, and Kyle and Maggie were working on baby number four.

Funny how much had changed in the last seven years or

so. He'd gone from a jaded, bitter man to a husband. To a father. Love had changed his entire universe. Not just the love he'd found with Cassie, but the love each of his brothers had found with their wives as well. His life was awash with nieces and nephews, with birthdays, and now that Nicholas, Maggie and Kyle's oldest, had started little kickers, soccer games on the weekends.

It was a good life. The life he knew down to his toes that he was supposed to be leading. And he was grateful.

Tonight though, he and his brothers had dates with their wives for a big open-air barbecue and dance down at the Grange Hall. And his parents' house would be filled with the next generation of Chases.

Yes, a date with his gorgeous wife, followed by some loud, blow-the-doors-off sex when they escaped early and in the morning too if he continued to be lucky.

Ward saw his cousins and nearly sprinted into the large living room his mother had turned into a wonderland for the ten-and-under set. Edward, chuckling, watched the retreat of his wife, and they both smiled at the sound of Polly Chase announcing cookies and milk while she read them all a story.

"Does your momma good to have all her grandbabies here. Not that I'm complaining, mind you. I happen to be the luckiest grandpa around. That and your momma is sexy when she's babying all those Chases."

"You sure you two can handle the full brunt of Chase kids at the same time?"

"I survived you and your brothers, didn't I? If I can get through your teenage years, I can survive a night with a bunch of Chases in footie pajamas giggling and carrying on. Two of us and eight of them. That's four half pints each. Your aunt may be coming over later, you know how she and your momma get with all these babies. Go on." His father took Ward's little overnight bag. "Enjoy the alone time with Cassie. I told your brothers all the exact same thing when they dropped babies off here."

Shane went in and was immediately swamped by tiny hugs and lots of calls of his name. Nicholas somberly assured him he was helping Grammy with the babies so they'd be fine. That and his mother had the magic touch with people large and small.

This was his life and damn it was good. This new generation of Chases his brothers had made with their wives would make their mark in the world. He liked that very much.

Cassie tucked a dahlia in her hair and took one last look at herself in the full-length mirror on the bedroom door. It'd been months since she'd been able to break away with Shane for a date. As much as she loved being a mother, and she did, she missed the time when she could focus on her relationship with Shane.

So when the Grange announced that they were going to have a barbecue and dance outside under the stars this year, Polly Chase had insisted she wanted all the Chase babies deposited on her doorstep and for each of her sons to squire their wives out for the evening.

Some women had horrible mothers-in-law. Cassie had apparently suffered her fill of horrible people because her mother-in-law was incredible. Loving. Supportive. She was a great example and a fabulous grandmother.

And she, together with her equally wonderful husband, Edward, had raised four of the finest men Cassie had ever known.

As if he'd heard her thoughts, Shane showed up in the doorway, a dozen red roses in his hands, looking handsome and sexy and appropriately interested and fascinated by the work she'd put into her hair, clothes and makeup.

He made her feel beautiful in a way no one else ever had.

He held the roses out. "Well hello there, Mrs. Chase. You're looking mighty delicious this evening."

She took the flowers, bending to press her face into them. It wasn't that he never did thoughtful things for her. He did. All the time as it happened. And yet it caught in her throat sometimes, the depth of what this man had brought to her life.

For years she'd lived in fear of her first husband. He'd hit at her, physically and emotionally, and he'd turned her into a person she couldn't face. She'd been someone she didn't respect. She'd escaped, running long and fast, and hadn't been in town more than five minutes before she'd been rear-ended by her crazy, big-haired, big-hearted mother-in-law. And through that moment she'd found Shane, who had helped her bring back the woman she was supposed to be.

He was big and bossy, grumpy at times, fussy when he didn't get his way. And gentle, loyal, attentive, protective and totally, utterly supportive. Here she was, years later, a wife and a mother, and she never could have imagined just how happy her life was.

"Hey." Seeing the emotion on her features, he took the roses and pulled her close. "What's wrong?"

She shook her head, swallowing back the emotion that'd swamped her for long moments. "Not a thing. It's all totally right. You make everything all right. Every day."

He rumbled deep in his chest, in that way he did sometimes when he struggled with his emotions. "I love you."

She hugged him tighter. "I love you too."

"We could skip the dance altogether."

She laughed. "Don't make offers you don't mean. You'd be into it at first and then start feeling guilty that people were expecting us." He didn't just take care of her and Ward, he took care of everyone, it was what he did. And why she loved him so much.

"I think I can make an exception for sex."

She tipped her head back to look up at him. Into that face of his she loved so much. "Oh, there'll be sex, mister. You can squire me around first. And then we can get to the sex part when we leave early."

He grinned. "All right then. Let's get to getting so we can get to leaving."

Chapter Two

Nathan raised a fist to knock on Lily's front door, but he wasn't ready for the breathtaking sight that presented itself when she opened up.

There she was, the first and only woman he'd ever given his heart to. Her smile kicked up a thousand watts when she saw it was him, and that filled him with joy enough to sweep her into his arms and kiss the hell out of her.

She pressed against him, those curves of hers teasing his senses. He sank into her, enjoying the fact that she was so very his.

When he broke away, he tipped his forehead to hers. "Good evening, Mizz Travis."

"Hi there. I certainly hope you don't greet everyone you know this way." She frowned and he laughed, kissing her one last time before stepping back.

"Of course not. Only the women I'm going to be marrying in five months' time."

He paused to smile the smile of a very satisfied man. Yes indeed, by year's end they'd finally be married. Life was good.

"Lucky girls." She stood to the side. "Come in before the neighbors call the police and Shane has to come arrest us."

Her younger brother, Chris, the reason she'd come back to Petal, slouched at the table. When he saw Nathan, he sat up straighter. It was in little acts like that when Nathan really saw the change in the boy since Lily had taken over the job of raising him.

Not even a year before Nathan wasn't convinced the kid would finish his sophomore year. Their mother had lost control of him and had begun to sink into a world numbed by alcohol and pills.

Lily had given up her job and her life in Macon and returned, and in the end had saved her mother, as well as her brother.

"Hey, Nathan." Chris stood and cleared his plate and cup. He'd come back from his wilderness camp a month prior, tanned and with the right attitude. He'd earned himself a spot on the high school marching band and had taken on a better circle of friends than the ones he'd gotten in so much trouble with before.

"Do you have gas money?" Lily spoke from where she'd returned from her bedroom with her bag. Nathan stared at her a while just because he could. Her hair was twisted up into a pretty knot, leaving her neck bare in the pale pink sundress she wore. It wasn't tight. It wasn't lascivious. It fit her perfectly, seeming to float around her as she walked.

All that sweetness only made the spice just beneath sexier.

"A twenty would be much appreciated." Chris sent his sister puppy dog eyes. Nathan recognized the look from his own siblings.

"You can use the gas card." She dug into her bag and handed him forty bucks. "In case you guys get pizza like you did last time. You did a good job on the lawn."

"Thanks." He grinned at her praise, and Lily couldn't help herself, she moved close enough to hug him and kiss his cheek. Quickly of course, as he was getting too old for the mushy stuff, as he'd informed her a few months back.

"I expect to see you back here by noon or so tomorrow. I

spoke to Mrs. Capwell earlier, she said to bring your swim trunks." It was also a way for her to underline that she was keeping tabs on him. She'd talked to the mom hosting this sleepover so he'd better not try to say he'd be one place and actually go another.

He'd come a long way from the boy he'd been when she first arrived back in Petal, but she had no plans to let him backslide. He'd done a lot to earn her trust again, but it wouldn't stop her from knowing where he was, when he was and who he was with. Her mother couldn't do the job, her father didn't want to, and as it happened, she loved Chris enough to know he was worth it.

"Who all's gonna be in the car with you?"

She nearly laughed aloud when she saw the look on Nathan's face at her horrible grammar. "By that I mean, who will you be giving rides to? I don't want you motoring around with a car full of teenage boys." She shuddered at the thought.

"Nah, it's cool. I'm picking Mike up on the way over but then we're in for the night. Mrs. Capwell got a bunch of movies, Sam said. We're eating and swimming and stuff."

"Okay then. Call if you need anything. I'll have my cell with me tonight."

"I'll see you tomorrow." He tucked the money into his pocket, hefted his duffle bag and headed out before she decided to try to kiss him or something.

And when he was gone she realized the dread that'd lived in her belly since she'd first come back had long since left her. Oh she'd keep an eye on him to make sure he didn't go back to his old ways. But she could trust him. And that meant so much.

Nathan grabbed her and kissed her again. "Now then. I feel like I've properly told you how much I've missed you."

When Chris had been at his wilderness camp and her

mother had been in detox and rehab, they'd had alone time. Sweet, blessed alone time to wander around his house totally naked and have sexytimes on any and all surfaces. But now that Chris was back and now that her mother had chosen to enter a longer-term treatment facility, alone time was a limited good.

Nathan had been so sweet about it, but she knew he chafed at that loss of freedom too.

"You saw me yesterday so don't pout. I have to reapply my lipstick now." She smirked, letting him know it wasn't a chore.

"Bubble gum. I don't think I've tasted bubble gum lip gloss after a kiss since the tenth grade."

She waggled her brows and quickly put the gloss back on.

"I want to see you every day." He brushed a kiss over her forehead. "I like waking up with you. I like seeing you at breakfast. I'm greedy that way."

Love swamped her. He had a way of getting past all her defenses, and she couldn't have stopped him even if she'd wanted to. "Me too. You're very handy to have around and you don't hog the covers."

"These months until the wedding can't move fast enough." He took a deep breath. "Now, you ready to look pretty on my arm?"

She grabbed her bag and took the arm he'd extended. "And I'm available for any feels you feel compelled to cop."

"Win/win for me, sugar. I'm a lucky, lucky man. I've got my bag in the car. Along with a peach cobbler Tate sent with me. I'll be right back."

Anticipation and joy washed over her at the mention of the cobbler—maybe even more excitement than when he'd said he liked waking up with her. The woman was totally easy for pie and cobbler.

"You're staying over?" She wanted him too. So very much. At first she'd been hesitant to let him stay over once Chris had returned, but he seemed to calm at the sight of Nathan, at knowing she was involved with someone stable and an authority figure in his life.

"Course I am. I like waking up next to you. You know Chris is aware we have sex. We're getting married and everything. Tomorrow if I had my way about it."

She paused. They'd had a little friction on this point, but she felt strongly over it. Growing up in his horrible household, he'd been thrust into a fatherhood role to help raise his siblings. She didn't want to take advantage of him like that. Chris wasn't his to raise. Nathan had a very full life with lots of people he took care of, and she didn't want to add more. It wasn't fair to him and it wasn't fair to Chris.

"I have to take him to the orthodontist tomorrow afternoon."

"I know. I'm going to take you both to lunch after." He took her hands. "What is it that makes you have that look on your face? Hmm?"

"He's not your responsibility."

He grinned in that way of his that sort of made it hard to keep her thoughts and wits about her. "We talked about this. He's not my responsibility, no. But he's yours and I like the kid and I love you. So I help, not because I'm obligated to, but because that's what you do when you're family. I'm your family, Lil."

"You have enough obligations in your life."

"I surely do." He laughed and hugged her, not missing the chance to give her butt a squeeze since they were alone and all. The rogue. "But you're not one of them and neither is Chris.

You're a pleasure."

She frowned. "You already raised your brothers and sisters. I don't want your relationship with me to be that."

He drew her to the couch and made her sit with him. "Lil, my childhood was a fucking nightmare. You know that. The only thing that saved me, saved us all, was the fact that we stuck together. I love how you are with your brother. I love that despite the fact that your mother and father both have checked out from parenting Chris, you haven't. It's one of the many reasons I love you the way I do."

Lily sighed, blowing it out and hoping some of her stress went with it. "She hasn't checked out. She's getting help. It takes time to relearn how to live your life."

"Good thing she's got her one responsible daughter to do her job then, because Chris can't just check out for six months in the meantime."

His mouth flattened into a line as he forced himself to stop speaking. She knew his feelings on the matter. Knew her mother's decision to spend six months in a group living situation two states away instead of nearer to her children had disappointed and angered him. But he'd been careful not to harp on it too much and she respected that.

Hell, she was pissed off enough on her own. But being pissed off didn't get Chris to the orthodontist. It didn't keep him out of trouble. And it wouldn't keep her mother sober either. Bitterness was a waste of time and she didn't have enough to waste.

He took her face in his hands and kissed her sweetly. "Baby doll, I love you. When you love someone, what they think is important is important to you too. If I felt put upon I would say so. Stop pushing me away. I'm not going anywhere. You're going to be my wife and the mother of my children. Helping you is not only what I'm supposed to do, but my pleasure. You're pretty independent as it is. I don't get too many chances to take care of things for you. It's really about me, you know."

She sighed, squeezing his hands. "I'm sorry I push you away sometimes."

He knew what it was like to be made to feel as if you were a burden. He knew she went out of her way to be sure Chris never felt that.

"Your father is full of crap. So's mine. I'd despair at all the worthless dads in the world if it weren't for those men who did such a great job at it like Edward Chase. *I'm your man.* You can't push me away because I'm not going to let you. Because I love you. Now. I'm staying over and you can make me pancakes in the morning to thank me. That together with some loud sex tonight when we get back should pay your bill in full."

Her face lost the tightness around her features as she smiled. "I don't know what I did to deserve you, Nathan Murphy."

The absurdity of this made him bark a surprised laugh. Given their history, the way it had been she who'd saved him instead of the other way around struck hard.

"I'm gonna put moves on you tonight you've never seen. Also, you're a miracle to me so be quiet and accept that graciously." He stood and held his hand out.

She took it and allowed him to draw her close again. "I can see I need to invest in some of that no-smudge lipstick or gloss. You're a menace to my lips."

He kissed her hard, bubble gum gloss and all.

Chapter Three

The lights in the trees and along the arbors around the dance floor lent the not usually very glamorous Grange some romance.

The scent of jasmine hung in the air, and Nathan thanked heaven for the breeze and the cleverly placed fans for keeping the place from being sweltering. Sweltering would have meant less opportunity to get nice and close to Lily on the dance floor.

And as delicious as she looked, he didn't want to waste a moment.

Currently, she sat across from him, her head bent toward his sister Beth as they laughed about something or other. Didn't matter what, he just liked to look at her. Liked to see her there with their friends and family.

"I hear you two finally set a date." Maggie Chase leaned across her husband Kyle to squeeze Lily's hand. "Polly has been talking about it nonstop."

"I really can't believe she's offering to let us use the house. It's far too generous. But she wouldn't take no for an answer."

The entire table erupted with laughter. Everyone who knew Polly Chase knew she didn't take no for an answer when she wanted the answer to be yes. She was a tiny woman with a will bigger than most he'd ever come across.

Nathan knew, much as Maggie would have, that Polly considered the Murphys part of her family, and once Polly considered you family, that was that. She'd see an offer of their house for the wedding as something to do because she'd do the same for her biological children.

Maggie looked to her husband a moment before looking back to Lily. "We got married there, so did Liv and Marc. It's a perfect spot. And you know Polly will love helping. She wouldn't have offered if she hadn't meant it."

Lily smiled and Nathan's chest tightened with emotion at the sight of the tears glimmering in her eyes. "She told me you all had a history of Christmas weddings and proposals, and she'd love for us to add to that tradition. She knows how to make a girl cry."

"I'm just relieved we have a date at last and a place. She can't run out on me now." He sent her a smile and she sent him one back, warming him all over. It was really time to go. Time to get her home and alone to divest her of all those clothes she had on. He wondered what her panties looked like and then realized he'd know all up close and personal-like very soon.

She blushed, probably knowing he was thinking dirty things about her. "Ha. You think I'd give you up now that you're all trained and stuff? I'm no fool."

"As guys go he's not bad." Beth tossed a beer-bottle cap at Nathan's head. Tate laughed.

"So guess what? I stopped by the Honey Bear earlier today, and William told me Joe Harris is coming back to Petal." Joe had been William's best friend back in the day. He'd been from the part of town Nathan and his siblings were. Joe had lived a hard life before he'd even turned eighteen. He'd been content to wild around getting in trouble, got arrested a few times for stupid, petty stuff. But he'd enlisted in the military and had turned his life around.

"I figured he'd go anywhere but Petal after he got out of the military." Nathan knew that feeling too.

"William said he was thinking about opening a business

here. He couldn't get really detailed, it was busy and the counter was overrun." Tate sat back against Matt.

Lily spoke to Nathan. "Get his contact info when you get the chance, Nathan. We need to invite him to the wedding."

Lily sent a look to Beth—a quick, sneaky girl look—and Nathan narrowed his gaze suspiciously.

Beth raised a brow and both women laughed.

"You didn't date him. I would have known." Nathan shook his head.

Lily laughed. "Oh goodness no. He was such a bad boy, my parents never would have let him up the front walk. But if I remember correctly, he's mighty cute, and from everything I've heard, he's changed his tune and turned his life around. Plus he's a friend of your brother's. It's welcoming, you know, to invite an old friend to a wedding."

"I agree. It's neighborly and all." Beth nodded, a smile edging her mouth, and Nathan looked toward Tate, who shrugged noncommittally, which meant she knew exactly what was up.

But when he looked back to Lily, she had that smile, the one she gave only to him, and suddenly nothing else mattered.

"I'm feeling a little tired." He said this looking straight at her.

"Yeah, me too."

Within moments everyone had gotten up and headed out to the parking lot. Hugs were exchanged as the husbands steered wives to cars.

"You know," Lily said as she buckled her seat belt, "we have all sorts of time. I don't think I've been out parking...well, ever."

"You think I know the best places to drive out into the

country? Hmm?" With a hand on her thigh, he pulled out onto the road and began to head away from Petal. "You think I'd know where to take a female for some smooching and a few bases?"

"I totally do, Nathan Murphy. You're a rogue. A handsome one at that. So I imagine you've taken a few ladies out to look at the stars while you were all smooth and got your hand up under their sweaters. They might have even let you put in the tip."

"Goddamn, Lil, you know what it does to me when you're this way."

She settled back against the seat with that smile of hers. "Oh yes, I surely do."

He drove, managing, just barely, to not break the speed limit. The last thing he wanted was to have this time with her interrupted by a ticket. Truth be told, he hadn't been out parking in a good fifteen years, but he was a high school teacher, after all. He'd heard the kids talking about this place or that place to go and make out. Pretty much the same places from when he was in high school.

She watched him as he drove, the window was down and her hair blew all over the place but she just pushed it back. He loved that she wasn't fussy, even as she was always so pretty and put together.

The road he took out to the lake wasn't as well maintained as the main one so he took it slow and finally found a good spot to park. The lake was down a hill and off in the distance. The moon was full and gave plenty of light.

Before he could say anything, she was in his lap and he had to push the seat back. "I'm not wearing any underpants. I put them in my purse an hour ago."

"Good Lord, woman, you're going to kill me." That he said

this as his hands busily skimmed up her thighs and under the skirt to find out if she was lying sort of negated the whole dying thing.

And yes indeed she was bare. Warm and wet, waiting for him. She gasped and then shivered when his fingers slid through her pussy, finding her clit and tickling it. Just a breath of a touch.

She squirmed and made that sound he loved so much. He skated his mouth down the line of her neck, and she held him to her, her fingers sliding into his hair and tugging.

"Demanding." He flicked open one of the buttons at the bodice of her dress and then another. "I'm going to take my time, so shush."

She laughed and leaned close enough to nip his ear and lick over the lobe. She knew it made him crazy. And it did.

"I love you, Lily." He took her mouth when she straightened to return the sentiment. She sighed into him, softening and letting him take the kiss wherever he wanted.

He tasted and teased, reveling in her, in that moment. Her tongue slid along his as she tasted and teased right back. They had amazing chemistry. He wanted her from the moment he woke up until the moment he fell asleep. Even with his hands on her, he wanted her. The need for what they did together, the energy they made, the way she filled his life excited him.

Impatient, she took matters in her own hands and unbuckled and unzipped his jeans, bringing his cock out. He started to argue, but why? Why complain when she rose up enough to slide herself down on his cock, taking him inside fully.

"That's so much better." She spoke into his mouth as he smiled.

"Mighty forward, ma'am. I am helpless against your filthy

183

urges."

This made her laugh. "Hush now. We can't get this truck rocking or we'll attract attention. So I'll do my best to keep my movement...internal." She showed him what she meant as she squeezed around him, jutting her hips a little and then back.

It was the illicit nature of the encounter, coupled with the heat of her, that tight embrace and the slide of her around his cock, that shredded his control.

"Just so you know, I'm going to fuck you again when we get home." His fingers got busy on her clit and she squealed.

"I'm counting on it. You do have some mighty fine recovery time. What girl wouldn't like that?" She braced her hands on his shoulders and pressed down on him, taking him in so deep he saw stars.

"I have the best fiancée in the whole damned world."

She laughed again but then gusted a curse when he increased the pressure of his fingers against her. Her pussy tightened around him and he knew it wouldn't be long for either of them.

And when she fell over the edge, she leaned forward and sank her teeth into his shoulder to keep from crying out. Which only made him hotter for her. Pushing him over right with her.

"I suppose some might think it's crazy to get down out here when we have the house all to ourselves," she said sleepily.

"Some don't have gorgeous, sexy women who'll take their panties off and give their men the night of their lives in a pickup just like they were teenagers again."

She appeared to be in no hurry to leave so he held her there on his lap, her body against his, still inside as their heartbeats slowed to normal again.

"I love you, Nathan."

He smiled against her hair. "I sure am glad."

Chapter Four

Matt pulled into the garage and sighed happily when he turned the engine off. "Just me and you, Venus. Hear that utter quiet?"

He got out and she met him, taking his hand as they went into the house. "Note it. It's such a rarity."

He spun her into his embrace. Her hair spilled around in a shower of pale moonlight. Her skirt flared as well, giving him a great view of her legs and those sexy-as-sin high heels she had a penchant for.

"I noticed something tonight."

She laughed, heading toward their bedroom, stepping around the toys, books and other flotsam that came with having kids.

"My new bra?" She said this as she tossed it to him, her blouse dangling from her free hand.

He caught up to her quickly, getting in close and taking a handful of those beautiful breasts. "Not until now. I tend to always be thinking about your breasts on some level. I did notice the way you jiggled when you danced tonight."

He pinched her nipples and she squeaked her approval. He spun her and backed her up to their bed.

"I haven't had you alone in this house in so long I don't even know." He bumped her back to the mattress, and she smiled up at him, topless and totally his.

"It's probably a good thing since you knock me up every

time we get alone."

He laughed as he pulled his shirt and jeans off and managed to get totally naked before he leapt on her like the feast she was.

He moved closer and unzipped the side of her skirt, sliding it down and off. The panties were deep blue, and they were so pretty against her pale skin he nearly hated to take them off.

But he did, tossing them over his left shoulder.

"What I did notice, aside from that new shade of lipstick you have on—and that I do like very much." He leaned down to kiss her quickly. "I noticed you didn't have a beer. Not a margarita either. No. I noticed you were drinking ginger ale. You rarely drink ginger ale. In fact, there are only a few times you do." Her smile grew as his heart pounded.

"I was going to tell you tomorrow. I didn't even know myself until this afternoon. I had a doctor's appointment two weeks ago. MaryAnn Twombly called me, she's the nurse in my doctor's office you see. You know her probably. She's one of those cheerleadery types you used to think were so great." She went about her story in the way she had, complete with little asides about everyone and everything. "So they ran a battery of tests on a sample I gave. I don't even know why they made me pee in a cup. I hate that."

He burst out laughing. "Sugar, is this your way of telling me you're having a baby?"

She nipped his lip when he came in for a kiss, pulling him down to her. "Yes."

"Hot damn, you're making me a daddy again." He kissed her once more, this time settling in for a long, slow smooch, her mouth open against his, the taste of her something he'd never tire of.

"You did have a little to do with it."

"I did, more than a few times."

She laughed and pulled him close before shoving him on his back and climbing atop his body.

All that pretty, moonlight-pale hair spilled around her bare shoulders, long enough to play peek-a-boo with her nipples.

"You're not feeling sick anymore?" He slid his palms up her sides, over skin so soft and pliant, over a body he knew every inch of but never ceased to appeal to him.

"Same as with the other pregnancies. I only feel woozy for an hour or so in the evenings and then I'm fine. I'm nearly two months along now. Thought I had the flu." She laughed and love filled him to bursting.

"Then it's safe to ravish you?"

"I'm always up for being ravished by you, Matthew Chase."

To underline her point, she went to her knees, reached around and guided him true and sank down again, taking him deep and stealing his breath.

"Damn, sugar, that feels fabulous." An understatement of course.

Tate should have known he'd be thrilled by her announcement. She should have known he'd notice she was drinking ginger ale. He kept a close eye on all those he loved, especially his women, as he referred to her and their daughters.

His concern always touched her. His excitement at the idea of adding another child to their family only reinforced that she was the luckiest woman on earth. This baby she carried would grow up in a house filled with love and joy, where he or she was wanted. That she could give that to her children was one of the best things she'd ever achieved. She'd come so far, had been blessed with so much it sometimes made her stop, her heart pounding, a smile on her face and tears blurring her vision.

All because of the man she loved. *The man who loved her.*

But right then it was just the two of them. Alone. Naked. She had far better things to do with her time and his body than getting weepy.

He was thick inside her. Hard. Insistent. That laid-back thing he did on the outside hid the less-than-laid-back realities of Matt Chase in bed. That man liked things his way. She smiled down at him and began to move, slowly at first, simply enjoying the moment. Knowing he'd strain to let her be in charge before finally taking over.

As games went, it was one of her favorites.

"That smile on your face should scare me. But I know you well enough to understand it's gonna be good for me either way."

She laughed and added a swivel, delighting in his grunt and the flush on his face.

"You feeling okay?"

So sweet. She nodded. "Better than okay." She pointed to him. "Hello."

His expression changed, and after a dizzy movement she found herself on her back with him looming over her. "That's better. Not that I don't love the way you look above me like the goddess you are. But this way...well." He waggled his brows and underlined his words by thrusting in deep and hard.

With her first pregnancy he'd been careful with her. She'd practically had to jump on him to get any action. He had been afraid to hurt her. Ha. But this was baby number three, and he'd learned she wasn't so fragile and that if he was hurting her she'd tell him just that.

Plus she knew he couldn't resist her, which was the most powerful aphrodisiac ever.

Another lucky thing was how good the man was with all his parts. He kept his pace relentless, but enough to hold back from climax. He could tease her for long periods of time, rendering her into an incoherent, begging mess.

"I love you, Tate." He bent to kiss her and she stretched up to meet his mouth.

"Love you too. Now make me come."

He laughed but moved to obey, his hand caressing her thigh to reach her clit, giving her a feather-light touch. Still, enough to send jolts of pleasure arcing through her system. Enough to make her inner walls clutch him tight.

"Damn," he snarled, and the touch on her clit became more sure.

He continued to devastate her until he had indeed turned her into an incoherent mess, just dancing right on the edge of climax. And he looked like a model while he did it. She was lucky.

"Now I think I'm ready to fly apart with you, darlin'." He said this as his touch firmed and that edge she'd been on sent her teetering over, headlong into orgasm so intense there was nothing but the two of them, nothing but his body against her, inside of her.

He followed with a snarl of her name.

When he fell to the bed with a happy sigh, she snuggled into his side, her arm over his chest.

"I'm a fortunate man to have you as my woman. First, you're sexier than all get out. Secondly, you're the finest cook ever. Thirdly, you make me laugh. You're good to my crazy family. I have to stop numbering because there are too many things. You listen to people. You make us all feel safe and loved. And you fill our house with our babies, mothering them so well. I know those girls aren't always easy to manage, but you do it.

190

And you do it in a way that makes it look effortless. Thank you."

She blinked back tears. "You're going to make me cry."

He chuckled. "I seem to recall you do that a lot when you're in a family way."

This was true. Everything seemed to make her cry when she was pregnant. Cotton commercials, dog-food commercials, sunsets, sirloin on sale at the market, didn't really matter. Everyone made allowances for it, which she found sweetly infuriating, and that made her cry too.

"You're the best thing that ever happened to me. And I still watch my morning visual donut when you go to work early and I'm in the shop."

He laughed at the reference to her daily ritual of sitting at the window of her hair salon and drinking her coffee, waiting to watch him walk from his car across the street to the fire station. It still made her happy to do it. Knowing that long, lean body of his was hers to touch and kiss. Knowing they'd made something real and deep. Knowing she'd be at his side for each graduation, each first date and prom, all the things they shared with their daughters.

Every day she had with him was a gift.

About the Author

To learn more about Lauren Dane, please visit www.laurendane.com. Send an email to Lauren at laurendane@laurendane.com or stop by her message board to join in the fun with other readers as well. www.laurendane.com/messageboard

Matt is an expert and the Chase is on.
Tate doesn't stand a chance.

Making Chase
© 2007 Lauren Dane

Tate Murphy is a girl from the wrong side of the tracks. She grew up a million miles away from the easy life Matt Chase has had. She's spent her life pulling herself and her siblings up and out of that trailer by the railroad tracks, and she hasn't looked back. Matt Chase is a dream of a guy, and she's certainly not going to turn down a short fling with one of the most handsome men she's ever seen!

Matt Chase has watched each one of his brothers find love and he knows he's ready for that too. It's all a matter of finding the woman who captures his heart. He's certainly sampled his fair share of them, but none has moved him the way Tate Murphy does when he goes to her shop to thank her for some cookies and a thank-you note.

But as Matt gets to know Tate and appreciate her strength and unique beauty, he also realizes she's got some big self-esteem issues about her past. To build a future, he's got to find a way past some big roadblocks.

Warning: this title contains the following: explicit sex, graphic language, some violence.

Available now in ebook and print from Samhain Publishing.

Enjoy the following excerpt for Making Chase:

He plopped down onto her couch and she stopped, looking at him, surprised. "What?"

"Yeah, not so good with the woo am I? I'd love for you to come here and sit with me."

Tate didn't know quite what to do. Matt Chase flustered the hell out of her. A sense of unreality settled into her. The guy, the donut of her dreams sat on her couch and wanted to kiss her? Did she hear him right?

"Tate? Did I say something to upset you? I want more than a kiss." He stopped and shook his head. "What I mean is I want to take you out too. This isn't just some fun way to spend my Sunday. Although, I'm certainly enjoying being with you. God, I'm usually more smooth than this," he mumbled and she laughed, kicking off her shoes and moving to the couch.

"I don't know what to say."

Scooting so that his body pressed full against hers, he put a finger over her lips. "Then don't say anything just now. I really need to kiss you, Tate. So I'm gonna."

His hand slid up her arm and cupped her neck, holding her, tipping her chin up. Before she had much of a chance to register anything but the delicious heat of his palm, his lips found hers.

Slow. Incrementally building up the heat, he gently led her to open up to his tongue. She'd never been really crazy about kissing but she realized it was just that she'd never been kissed by someone who knew what he was about before. All the difference in the world lay right there.

He didn't jam his tongue in her mouth and down her throat, he teased her with it, tasted her, tickled her with the tip. His teeth joined the action, coming in to nip her bottom lip from time to time until she nearly panted with wanting him more.

The heat of his mouth moved from her lips, skating along her jaw to the hollow just below her ear. A gasp ripped from her gut when he sucked there, the wet, warm sensation shooting straight to her nipples and then to her pussy, flooding her with moisture.

Needing more of him, she adjusted, sliding her hands up into his hair.

Matt had never wanted a woman more than he did as the taste of her rushed through him. She was soft under his hands, smelled right, felt good. These little sounds kept coming from her, little moans and sighs of need, and it drove him crazy. He didn't want to scare her but if he didn't get inside of her sometime soon his cock would explode.

Before he knew it, her hands had slid from his hair to his chest and she was opening the front of his uniform shirt. Hesitantly but with some strength, she pushed him back enough to get on her knees and part the front of his shirt. When she leaned down to brush kisses over his collarbone before moving to flick a tongue over his nipples, he jumped, breathing her name like a prayer.

Her hair was like silk over his superheated skin. Needing to see it all, he reached back and undid the clasp holding it up. It tumbled down in a sweet-smelling wave.

When one of her hands slid down his belly and her nails scored over his cock he moved back into action.

He took her arms so he could see in her face. What greeted him, passion-glazed eyes and kiss-swollen lips, made him suck in a breath. Holy shit she was beautiful.

"Tate, I want you. Are you with me?"

Swallowing, she nodded before licking her lips.

"Bedroom?"

She stood, held out a hand and led him toward the back of the house. He felt her tremble a bit, but as he was shaking too, it was hard to tell where he began and she ended.

Her room was messy and it made him smile.

"God, I'm sorry. I...well it goes without saying I wasn't expecting to bring a man back here." She motioned toward her unmade bed and turned out the light he'd turned on.

For some reason, that comment only made him want her more.

"Good." He used his body to push her toward her bed until she fell back and looked up at him, her hair a brilliant corona around her head. "Tate, I want to see you." He turned on the bedside lamp before moving to unbutton the bodice of the dress she wore.

The blush was back and she put her hands over his, stilling them. "Turn the light off, please."

"But I won't be able to see you that way. Tate, I've been fantasizing nonstop about your body for weeks now."

"I can't. Matt, please."

Instead of turning the light off, he lay down on the bed and pulled her to him. "Tate, are you changing your mind about making love to me?" She shook her head but he saw the glimmer of tears in her eyes. "What is it, sweetness? Am I scaring you? Moving too fast?"

She buried her face in his neck and he burrowed through her hair to hold her. "I don't want you to see me naked."

"If you're not naked, how can I be inside you?" That's when it occurred to him he didn't have any condoms.

"Just leave the lights off!"

"Tate, I want to see you. Would you deny me that pleasure?" He pulled his head back to see her face, hoping she'd smile but he got confusion, anger and a bit of embarrassment too. What the fuck? "Tate? What is it?"

She pushed at him and jumped up, pacing in front of the bed. "I'm not one of the women you're normally with!"

"I know."

She stopped and sneered.

"I mean," he added quickly, "yes, you're not like them. And that's a *good* thing. Tate, you're important, special."

"Matt," she sighed, sounding impatient. "Are you going to make me spell it out?"

"You'd better, sweetness, because I have no fucking idea what the issue is."

"Dolly, Melanie, Lisa, Kelly—what do these things have in common and what do I not have that they do?"

"They're vapid and shallow and you're not?" Standing and going to her, he kissed her lips quickly, tossing his shirt to one side blindly.

"Okay, well, you have a point there. Although what the hell were you doing with them if so?" The air left her lips in a soft whoosh when he pushed her gently back down to the bed.

"Well you have a point there too. We can talk about the ramifications of that later because it's totally getting in the way of me putting my cock into your body. And speaking of that, we're not getting naked again why?"

"Because you go out with women who are drop-dead gorgeous and I am not! They're all tall and thin and *cheerleaders*. I am, aside from having breasts and a vagina, nothing like them."

He tried not to laugh, he really did but she was hilarious.

"What are you laughing at?"

He rolled and pinned her to the bed with his body, raining

kisses down her chest, over the fabric of her dress. Pulling her skirt up, he traced the soft skin of her thighs with his fingertips.

"I'm laughing at you, Tate Murphy. I've never heard anyone but Maggie say cheerleader like it was some sort of disease. Frankly, I find it hard to find fault with women jumping around in tight sweaters and short skirts but I don't think it has a damned thing to do with why I'm dying here for you and not with anyone else. I'm here because *you're* here. I don't want them, I want you. I want to see your body, I think you're beautiful."

"I can't concentrate with the lights on."

There was so much panic and emotion in her voice he let it go. Reaching out, he turned out the light.

"Better?"

"Yes."

He found her mouth again and she relaxed, melting into him, hooking one of her thighs around his ass, arching her back to bring her pussy into contact with his cock.

Busy hands found the buttons on her bodice and made quick work of them, exposing her bra to him. He wished he could see more in the dim light that came from the open bedroom door but there'd be time for that later.

There wasn't a catch between her breasts so he helped her to sit up to get the back hooks undone.

Sweet mercy, her breasts, even what he could see in the low light, were beautiful. Large, heavy, juicy, dark nipples.

While she sat up, he helped her get the dress off and tossed his pants, socks and boxers before returning to her. She'd slid under the sheets, which agitated him, but he began to really understand some of what Liv had said a few weeks before about what some people might think about Tate. Apparently Tate herself felt some of those things too. Well, that'd be next, showing her just how damned beautiful she was—cheerleader or not.

When their bodies came together, skin to skin he thought he'd lose consciousness it was so deliriously good. Fuck! Condom.

"Tate, uh, I have a problem. *Shit!*" She grasped his cock, giving a few slow pumps with her fist.

"What is it?" She nibbled on his ear and he lost his train of thought for long moments until she smeared her thumb over the wet slit at the head of his cock.

"Condom. I don't have one. Please, please tell me you do." He caught a nipple between his lips, swirling his tongue around it.

"I, ohgod, I don't. I don't bring men back here for sex."

He rested his forehead on her chest a moment, disappointed but not in her comment that she didn't bring men back for sex. "Okay, well I'm not leaving to go get one either. We'll just work around it. We can do other things for tonight."

"Other things? Oh, yesss."

SAMHAIN

PUBLISHING

It's all about the story...

Romance

HORROR

Retro
ROMANCE

www.samhainpublishing.com

CPSIA information can be obtained at www.ICGtesting.com
Printed in the USA
LVOW061031231212

312972LV00003B/231/P